THE CORONA BOOK OF
HORROR STORIES

THE CORONA BOOK OF
HORROR STORIES

edited by
LEWIS WILLIAMS

CORONA
BOOKS

First published in the United Kingdom in 2017

by Corona Books UK
www.coronabooks.com

ISBN 978-0-9932472-6-2

Cover design by Martin Bushell
www.creatusadvertising.co.uk

CONTENTS

INTRODUCTION

This book has been a labour of love. At times, it seemed like an utterly crazy idea: to compile a book of horror stories comprising the best of unsung new writing in horror on a non-existent budget, and, to complicate the situation, to include amongst the contributors existing Corona Books authors whose genre isn't actually horror. There was even some scepticism that we could find enough good stories to fill the book. The sceptics were wrong. We received a fantastic response to the open call we held for submissions and were blown away by the quality of the stories we received. The overall standard of submissions was very high – there's a lot of writing talent out there, which mainstream publishers ignore! This left us with some difficult decisions to make and there were a number of very good stories that we received and didn't have space to include in the book. Thanks therefore go to everyone who submitted stories, whether or not their stories made the final cut. Closer to home, we asked our existing authors, already published or to be published by us, whether they would like to submit a story for the book. The following Corona authors whose writing isn't normally horror rose to the challenge and submitted stories we think more than deserve their inclusion here: Keith Trezise, Suzan St Maur and Philip Onions. There is also a brand new story from our very own master of modern macabre T.R. Hitchman, whose collection of ten dark and twisted tales, *Child of Winter*, we published last year. There is also a story included here by someone called Lewis Williams!

In compiling the book we've not only tried to bring you the best in horror writing, but to bring you variety (it being the spice of life). In this volume you will find a mix of natural and supernatural horror: some of the horror you'll find here is all too human in its source; some of the horror lies in forces beyond scientific understanding or the laws of nature. I won't tell you which stories fall into which category, lest that information spoils anything that lies in store for you. In some stories the horror is graphic; in others it is more the result of the suggestion of dark forces at work. There is temporal variety in the stories too. Most have a contemporary setting, but the stories by S.J. Menary, Suzan St Maur and A.H. Sargeant have, in part or in whole, historical settings; and Mark A. Smart's contribution is set in the near-future. There are shorter stories and longer stories – the longest is six times the length of the shortest. And there is geographical variety too. Most of the stories are set here in the UK, but Joanie Chevalier's and William Quincy Belle's contributions are not. With those stories from North American writers, their native spelling and grammar is preserved. Elsewhere this book is presented in British English (where we have colours, sceptics and centres rather than colors, skeptics and centers etc.) Wondra Vanian's story is something of a special case. Wondra is American, but I suggested we might set her story in Wales, where she has lived for 14 years, and she obliged. Her story is therefore the exception that proves the rule – a story by an American writer, but with British spelling.

In case of interest and to aid readers who might want to follow up on the stories they like best by seeking out other work by the same author, we've included at the end of the book some potted biographies of all the contributors. There is also a listing of websites and Twitter accounts for those authors who have them (and are happy for us to tell you what they are).

And who knows, if this book proves to be a big enough success, we might do it all again next year and there might be a *Second Corona Book of Horror Stories*. You, dear reader, can help the cause. If you enjoy this book, tell your friends, talk about it to strangers, review it on Amazon, shout it (metaphorically) from the rooftops. If enough of you do, I'll look forward to seeing you next year, same time, same place.

Lewis Williams

NIZZY'S EGG

S.L. Powell

When my friend Nizzy was a child he thought that living on a farm was the coolest thing in the world. And he was lucky in that respect, because he did spend a lot of his childhood on a farm. He lived there with his mum and dad and brothers and sisters, and his grandmother too. It was a wonderful life. Nizzy would get up just as the sun was peeping over the horizon, and go down to the milking shed where the cows were lined up waiting to go into their stalls. He would smell that lovely mixture of warm cows and hay and milk and fresh cow dung. He would drink milk that came straight from the cow and had eggs for breakfast that he'd just found in the henhouse. It was all bliss. But best of all were the chickens. Nizzy adored the chickens.

Chickens, of course, are birds, and birds are peculiar things, perhaps because they're descended from two-legged dinosaurs like the velociraptor or the Tyrannosaurus rex. Of course, birds have shrunk a bit since the days of the dinosaurs, but in other ways they still have a lot in common. Take their thin scaly legs, and the hooked claws on their toes. Even their feathers are a bit weird. I mean, they *seem* soft enough, but in fact they're tough and shiny. And then there's the really bizarre thing that's happened to the bird's mouth. Creepy. If birds were still two metres tall we'd be terrified of them, instead of thinking how pretty and cute they are with their fluffy feathers. Imagine the crow in the garden or the pigeon in the street towering over you, with a beak as long as a carving knife.

The other odd thing about birds is their eyes. Birds look as if they're staring all the time. This is because they don't have proper eyelids, and they don't blink in the way that we do. They don't have that nice droopy bit with a fringe of eyelashes that hangs over the eye, and makes other animals like dogs and sheep and cows and even elephants look almost human. Birds just – well, *stare*. Chickens and geese look especially odd because their eyes are often bright blue, or green, or golden brown, just like ours. But they don't blink. All that happens is that every now and again a filmy bit of skin flashes sideways across the eye to keep it clean. That's not blinking, if you ask me.

Nizzy loved those chickens, though. He loved everything about them, from the way they scraped for food in the dirt to the way they fluffed up their feathers when they sat in the henhouse at night. He loved the nervous little noises they made when anyone came too near. I didn't know Nizzy when he was a child, but I can imagine what he was like. Now he's grown up he's tall and gentle, with a soft, musical voice, and when he was a child I expect he was *small* and gentle, and his voice would have soothed the chickens and made them feel safe. I expect he used to crouch down and talk to them, and watch the way they cocked their heads and listened, staring at him, and slightly shaking those strange fleshy red crests on their heads.

All the children in Nizzy's family had little jobs to do on the farm, like bringing in the milk, or feeding the pigs and goats. Nizzy had a special job, which was perfect for him. It was to go out with a basket every morning and collect the eggs that the chickens had laid. He would go round the barns and the henhouses, looking carefully in every pile of straw, in every box, in every corner. Chickens will nest just about anywhere, and you have to have sharp eyes to spot all the eggs.

Nizzy was good at finding eggs. He knew all the likely places. There was one chicken who insisted on laying in the cowshed, right under the cows' feet, which meant she spent an awful lot of time squawking furiously at the cows as they ambled around. It also meant that her eggs often got smashed, but she never seemed to learn. There was another hen who regularly laid her eggs under an old horse trough at the bottom of a field. The horse trough was full of stinky green water, and toads lived under there, which the children always liked to talk to but they never answered back.

On his morning rounds Nizzy would gather all the eggs up carefully and put them in his basket, and when there were no more eggs to collect he took the basket back to the house. Then, every morning, he would sit down with his granny to a fine breakfast of soft-boiled eggs and toast soldiers. They always had two eggs each.

Nizzy was very happy with his chickens and his egg-collecting, but somehow it wasn't quite enough. He felt there was something missing. The 'something' was a cockerel. Nizzy *desperately* wanted a cockerel. He longed to see one strutting around the farmyard and showing off his fine feathers. He pleaded with his grandmother, who was in charge of the chickens.

'Oh, go on, Granny! He wouldn't be any trouble. I'd look after him.'

'You can't have a cockerel,' said his granny. 'They make too much noise. He'd crow at the crack of dawn. You'd be able to hear him in Bradford.'

'But we all get up at the crack of dawn anyway. And there isn't anyone else for miles. Oh please. Please. Please. They're so beautiful. And anyway you told me once that chickens don't fight so much if there's a cockerel around. They'd probably lay more eggs. *Please...*'

'I'll think about it,' said his granny, shortly. Her wrinkled face didn't give much away, and Nizzy gave up arguing.

As it happened, his grandmother's promise to think about it wasn't just soft soap to shut Nizzy up. She *did* think about it. And eventually decided Nizzy did deserve a cockerel. He was so good with those chickens, and never missed a day's egg-collecting.

The farmer next door had an ancient bantam cockerel that he wanted to get rid of. (In truth, he didn't it expect to live much longer.) So he gave him to Nizzy. Bantams are small chickens, so the cockerel was smaller than many of the chickens in the farmyard. But that didn't stop it bossing the chickens around. Cockerels are *incredibly* bossy. And this one was also vicious. He'd stab you in the hand if you dared to try to feed him, and would charge furiously at any visitors who wanted to enter the farmyard. Even Nizzy with his gentle voice couldn't tame him, and everyone else in the family thought the cockerel was a big fat nuisance.

Nizzy didn't care. He was so proud. He called the cockerel 'Cocky', which just about summed him up. Despite his age, Cocky was utterly beautiful, and he seemed to know it. He had every colour of the rainbow in his feathers, and marched up and down keeping the chickens under control and making a terrible noise.

One particular morning Nizzy went off before breakfast to collect the eggs as usual, and he found a chicken sitting in a place he'd never spotted before. She was tucked away almost out of sight in a corner of the barn, right behind the large frame of an old rusty bit of machinery that nobody used any more.

'What *are* you doing under there?' said Nizzy.

The chicken glared at him suspiciously, but she didn't budge. Her head twitched ever so slightly.

'I'm coming to get you, you know,' said Nizzy kindly. And he began to wriggle under the rusty machinery on his stomach.

The chicken wasn't happy, and made angry warning noises. 'Buk! Buk! Buk!'

'I won't hurt you,' said Nizzy. He was starting to wonder if *he* might be the one to get hurt. There wasn't much room under there and he was feeling a bit squashed. But as he edged closer, and the agitated chicken hopped off her nest and backed away, and Nizzy saw the eggs – then he forgot all about himself suddenly. There were *loads* of eggs, so many that Nizzy quickly lost count. He was very pleased with himself at finding such a haul. He put them one-by-one in his basket; it took ages, because he could hardly move under the big rusty whatever-it-was. The chicken hovered nearby, making a terrible fuss. She was still complaining (buk-buk-buk-buk-buk-BUUK!) when Nizzy was well on his way back to the farmhouse for breakfast.

And then, as usual, he washed his hands and laid the breakfast table, while his granny put four of the eggs on to boil, and made toast and buttered it, and cut it into soldiers ready for the marvellous moment when Nizzy could dunk it into his egg.

'How are you doing, Granny?' said Nizzy as he rummaged in the cutlery drawer.

'Hmmm,' said his granny.

Granny was a lady of few words when she was busy, so Nizzy just filled in the spaces himself.

'Oh, good,' he said. 'Listen, you wouldn't believe where I found a chicken today!'

'Hmmm,' said his granny.

She was so unresponsive sometimes, it was a bit like talking to the toads, but Nizzy didn't mind.

'She was right under that old rusty thingummybob in the barn. Right at the back.'

'Harrower,' said his granny.

'What?'

'Harrower, that's what it's called.'

'What's a harrower?'

'That thing in the barn,' said his granny, ending the explanation.

Nizzy gave up, and went back to his tale about the chicken.

'She didn't like it when I came for her. She had so many eggs! Did you see them all, Granny?' And Nizzy chattered on as he put the egg-cups, which were decorated with pictures of fluffy chicks, on the table.

And when Nizzy sat down to breakfast and the egg was ready, first of all he tapped the top of it with the back of his spoon, and then picked off the pieces of shell. He had to blow on his fingers every now and again, because the egg was hot. And then he took a spoonful of egg and popped it into his mouth, and pushed the toast finger down into the egg.

But there were two things that were a bit strange. Firstly, Nizzy could feel something hard and chewy in his mouth, like a bit of stale toast. He hadn't eaten any toast, though. What was it? Not eggshell, it wasn't crunchy enough. Then Nizzy looked at the toast finger that he'd just pulled out of his egg.

The end of the toast finger was red.

Funny, thought Nizzy. I've seen yolks that are nearly orange, but never a red one. He tried to take another spoonful out of the top of the egg. He thought he felt the spoon hit something hard in the middle of the egg. And when he looked down into the egg, he saw the most dreadful thing.

It was an eye.

The eye stared up at him from inside the egg. It didn't blink. It looked at him accusingly. And Nizzy realised with horror that the eggs he had collected from that chicken in the barn had been nearly ready to hatch. *He had soft-boiled a chick for breakfast.*

Needless to say, Nizzy has never eaten another egg in his life, whether boiled, fried, scrambled, poached or made into an omelette.

TICKS

Lewis Williams

I

'Samson! Samson!'

'Samson! *Samson!*'

'*Samson!* SAMSON!'

'SAMSON!'

'SAMSON!'

Both Rachel and Thomas were now shouting out their dog's name with quite some desperation.

'Where the fuck has he got to?'

'Thomas!' Rachel responded, with a tone that carried a meaningful reprimand for his language without the need for another word to be added. After eight years together as a couple, Rachel and Thomas were able to communicate a good deal of meaning and emotion to each other just by the way they said each other's names, whether they respectively chose to say 'Thomas', 'Tom' or 'Tommy', or 'Rachel' or 'Rach' and in what tone.

Their brief, bristling exchange reflected the fact that they both were now at the point of seriously beginning to panic. Dark was falling rapidly. Rachel had begun using the torch, that is the assistive light app, on her mobile several minutes ago, and that on top of the day's usage had all but drained the battery. Soon they would be in the woods in total darkness, having not seen their beloved Samson for what felt like an eternity, but was in reality a mere ten or twelve minutes.

'Look, let's get back to the car before we get lost ourselves, get a torch from home and come back to look for him properly, for as long as it takes. I mean, he's got to be somewhere.'

'Oh God, Tom, he's hurt or something. Or somebody's taken him. Do we go to the police?'

'If we can't find him when we come back, yes, I think we should. But I don't know how interested they'll be about a missing dog. They'll probably just take down the details and do nothing about it at all. I can see us putting up missing dog posters on every lamppost and telegraph pole between here and home.'

'And never see him again?' They held each other in a rare display of such affection outside the home, albeit as far as they were aware they were not in the sight of anyone else.

'I know, Rach. I love that dog as much as you do'

'That dog? He's got a name,' Rachel snapped back, breaking the intimacy. She doubted Thomas really did feel the same about Samson as she did.

'Come on, let's get back to the car.'

They disengaged and Thomas offered his hand to Rachel to hold as they walked.

'This way?' he asked.

'I think so.'

The well-trodden, muddy path they began to follow would indeed lead them out the woods and back to the piece of tarmac where their Peugeot estate was parked. But they had walked little further than a few metres along it, when a sound of movement made them turn around sharply.

Samson bounded back to them, panting, appearing stupidly cheerful as if to say *what were you worrying for?*

Rachel knelt to receive him, and hugged him and kissed him on the mouth as some dog owners are wont to do. Samson licked her face in return.

II

Dennis Stevens thought that people who kept dogs, cats or anything as pets that you could easily find in 'Pets at Home' on those ubiquitous out-of-town retail parks, showed a singular lack of imagination. Nature was a wonderful world of so many different creatures surviving in so many different ways that, say, keeping a dog and feeding it tinned food, or keeping a hamster and feeding it pet shop hamster food was just a dull and boring thing to do. Dennis's philosophy was that you only lived once and if you chose to spend that one life doing the same things that everybody else did in the same way that everybody else did, or that millions of other people did in the same way that millions of people did, that was a shocking waste of that life. Interests, interesting interests gave life a purpose and, well, interest. He recalled a conversation he once had with an acquaintance at work, Paul Turnbull, who had gone with his wife to see a mortgage advisor at the HSBC bank. The mortgage advisor had asked them questions and listened to them explain their lifestyle and their finances. After the interview the mortgage advisor wrote up the results in a report, as was her job to do, and that report included the line that Paul and his wife 'do not have any interests or hobbies outside work'. Paul had seemed most put out by that inclusion, but Dennis suspected it was true and that was why it left Paul rankled. The truth hurts. Paul had never struck Dennis as in any way being an interesting person.

Particular interests and hobbies were what made life worth living. You couldn't just go to work, come home, watch TV, rest, go to work again. Even if you added raising children and having sex with the wife occasionally to that list, it still didn't strike Dennis as appetising. It reminded him of the lyrics from what would probably always be his favourite ever song 'Racing in the Street' by Bruce Springsteen: 'Some guys they just give up living, and start dying little by little, piece by piece. Some guys come home from work and wash up and go racin' in the street'. The hero, or maybe anti-hero, of the song had an interest that kept him living, kept him from just dying slowly. That interest was auto street racing, illegal and high adrenalin, but to Dennis 'cars and girls' wasn't the point of that song; rather it was about doing what you had to do, doing what you do to make you feel alive because you can't do anything else. The genius of the song was to put existential angst so simply, so directly without complication. Dennis had never considered street racing as an option for him – it was anyway more of a cultural phenomenon to be found in the North-East states of 1970s America than it was in the East Midlands of 21st century England – but 'Racing in the Street' struck a chord with him every time he listened to it.

Dennis's interest in life couldn't have been more different to street racing. Dennis's particular interest was parasites.

He wasn't sure when this interest began to mean so much to him – he'd happily admit it to himself it was now an obsession – but he could trace its beginnings back to when he was a boy. His parents had two dogs, a long-haired black Alsatian and a brindle and white Bulldog. He hated them both. The Bulldog was literally neither use nor ornament, the latter because it was spectacularly ugly. Worse, it always seemed to smell musty and seemed completely incapable of sleeping without snoring obnoxiously. The Alsatian he found little more charming. Its habits included drinking out of the toilet and eating any faeces it would find in the street, whereupon it would rush back to its owners with – if dog's can be said to grin – a literally shit-eating grin on its stupid face. Both the dogs periodically had fleas. And because the fleas must have annoyed the dogs, the young Dennis liked and respected the fleas more than he did the dogs. He read up about them and found that they had a form far more interesting than that of a dog and a purity of purpose and natural design that astounded him. The dog flea, he discovered, lived on blood sucked from its host and had mouth parts adapted for piercing skin and sucking blood optimally. It could survive without such feeding for several months, and had, relative to its size, very long hind legs which enabled it to jump – again relative to its size – utterly spectacular distances to land on its host. Once on its host and having had its fill of blood, the female could lay up to an amazing 4,000 eggs to reside in its host's fur.

But the fleas just didn't bite the dogs; they bit Dennis too. For long swathes of his boyhood he could remember having flea bites. They mainly bit his lower legs. He could recall his calves being covered in bites, and he would scratch them as they itched like hell. They would then start to scab over and he would scratch them again, sometimes scratching so many nascent and established scabs so hard that the blood would run down his legs. His mother told him that if he caught one of the fleas, he should squash it between two finger nails as they were 'hardy little bastards' and that was the best way to kill them, and you'd know you'd killed them when you felt their hard, little, ruddy brown bodies give way under your finger nails as they flattened between them. But Dennis never did kill them; he respected them too much and they interested him too greatly.

III

'I'm so glad he came back, Tom. I don't know what I'd have done if we'd lost him. I don't think I'd have slept if I'd taken a dozen Nytol. I just couldn't've slept. I'd just have been willing someone to call or knock on the door saying they'd brought Samson home. I'm so glad we put our address and my mobile on his tag. You know, if it happens again; I couldn't bear it.' She paused before adding in less of a rush of words, 'I love that dog, you know.'

'More than you do me?' Thomas asked, perhaps only half joking.

'No, not more than I do you.' She stretched her arms out straight horizontally from her body, as if being crucified but with her fingers curled in just slightly so as to indicate measuring an imaginary distance. 'I love Samson this much, but I love you a little bit more.'

Excitement over and relief comforting them, Rachel and Thomas more or less settled back into their usual Saturday routine, involving a bottle of wine, sometimes a film, but more often, and tonight in particular, the BBC1 Saturday night TV schedule. Walking Samson in the woods together was the closest they got to going out together for the most part these days. Sometimes there was a lot of silence between them. Rachel would sometimes read whilst Thomas would watch television – especially if she was hooked on the story in the book she was reading. Thomas read less, if at all. He would argue that any decent story would be filmed or televised sooner or later and he could experience it that way without the inconvenience of having to read a book. The silences between them weren't uncomfortable, though. After eight years together, five years married, theirs wasn't a passionate love anymore. It was something different, calmer, more solid. They were both comfortable in each other's company without the need for giving each other attention all the time. It was something right; it was how it should be, except ... well, except there was no immediate prospect of them having children and each medical attempt they had made at beating their infertility just bought false hope and ultimately disappointment.

Rachel sometimes wondered if people took her fondness for Samson for her treating the dog as a child substitute. But it wasn't like that. One of Thomas's favourite guilty pleasures was re-watching episodes of the old sitcom *Only Fools and Horses* – he had them all on DVD – and Rachel quietly hated the characters of the childless couple Boycie and Marlene with the latter having a stupid little dog that the joke was she treated as a baby substitute. Well, Samson wasn't a girly little dog like that; he was a muscular 75lb long-haired black Alsatian. Moreover, it was natural for her to be very attached to Samson, as there had been a Delilah, a black and silver Alsatian bitch, that had been taken from them in the cruellest circumstances. When she was only about a year old, technically still a puppy and boundless with energy, they surmised Delilah must have escaped from a hole in the garden fence. She was returned to them dumped on their doorstep dead, again they surmised by a car driver too cowardly to own up to having run down their pet. Delilah didn't look injured – there was no blood or any gruesome injuries to see, just her lifeless body, still, unsettling in the way that all corpses are. Rachel had made the discovery of the body, and the horrible moment still haunted her to this day. The lightest she could ever be about the incident was to only half-jokingly blame Thomas for having given the dog that name that meant she got murdered – like the Delilah in that stupid Tom Jones song. Nevertheless, they had named Samson, Delilah's replacement, in tribute to her name. No, it was perfectly understandable that she should treasure Samson as much as she did.

That night, basking in the relief of Samson's return, Rachel and Thomas made love for the first time in nearly two weeks. The last thing on either of their minds was to check the dog's body for ticks as was Blue Cross recommended practice following a walk in the woods.

IV

With greater educational ability or a series of better life choices, Dennis Stevens might have become a biologist. As it was, he became a local government administration officer. He had at one point applied for a job at a university zoology department, albeit an admin one – he didn't have the qualifications for becoming a researcher himself. Had he got that job, it would have been life-changing. He would have moved to the other end of the country, for one thing. He didn't get the job. Correctly sensing at one point that the interview panel wanted him to mention biodiversity – the job was in part about supporting the outreach activities of the researchers and that was very much a key buzzword to them – he did so, but then went on to talk about the

Pthirus pubis, the pubic louse, and how it would be an awful thing if the current popularity amongst women of Brazilian waxing meant that the species died out. The panel couldn't have looked more surprised at this than if he had've got up and dropped ice cubes down their backs.

Disheartened, Dennis didn't persevere with any attempts to get a job related in any way to his overriding interest in life. Instead, parasites, specifically ectoparasites – those living outside their host's body – remained his private free-time interest, which obsession eventually came to displace almost all other interests in his life. He invested in magnifiers and microscopes. He collected specimens and learnt how to preserve them in clear casting resin. He experimented with parasite livestock, testing how long different varieties of parasite could survive away from their host. Fleas could survive well; head lice much less so. He was fascinated to be able to see sights such as the *Sarcoptes scabiei*, the scabies mite, under the microscope – its body appearing as a partly translucent blob with tiny legs like the short ends of worms' tails with twitching single hairs appearing to grow out from them; but Dennis's greatest passion was for parasites that could be seen with the naked eye, especially fleas and ticks. Yes, ticks were a particular favourite of his.

V

Rachel woke around 9am. It was Sunday; the alarm wasn't set, so she was able to wake up naturally in her own time. Thomas's space in the bed was empty. She wondered if he had gone out already. She envied him for being able to pull on a pair of trousers, put on shoes and a top and simply go out with no need to do anything with his short hair or put on makeup. Rachel wouldn't venture out the house without at least twenty minutes – fifteen minutes at an absolute push – to sort out her hair and makeup in preparation. Perhaps Thomas had gone to the Co-op to get fresh croissants. He did that sometimes on special occasions, and they would enjoy them warmed up – a few minutes in the oven was all it took – and served with strawberry jam. Divine. If so, she might even reward him with a sexual treat – if he was up to it after the previous night. A breakfast of strawberry jam followed by pearl jam, perhaps. She smiled to herself at her own little joke. Too fattening to have either very often, and in truth tasting the latter was something she did far more for Thomas's pleasure than her own, but it was a special occasion of sorts – Samson was safe after what had been a nasty scare. She called for Samson. Thomas would have already let Samson out, so there would be no urgency for her to get up and do that. She herself, of course, felt the need to urinate, but it wasn't an utterly urgent need. The thick curtains were still drawn in their bedroom and the room was still fairly dark. She could enjoy a 'snooze', a few more minutes in bed before getting up. She called again for Samson, a little more loudly this time. He heard her and came, but rather than bounding into the room and onto the bed as he might usually do, his approach was a bit more lackadaisical, and it almost seemed to be an effort for him to climb up onto the bed. Rachel received him and cupped his head in her hands. It was obvious something was wrong. Around his eyes were a series of what she first thought were warts, little bulbous misshapen brown berries that seemed to have ripened unnaturally overnight. How could she not have seen them last night? They were ticks. Much bigger than they would have been last night, true. Their bodies engorged with blood sucked from Samson. Then she properly noticed

Samson's ears, the insides of which were filled with the same disgusting blood-filled brown berries, what seemed like hundreds of them, some bigger and lighter brown than others as if their bodies had taken in blood to their bursting point. Rachel felt sick, repulsed from Samson by the abhorrence of the sight, the feel, the very presence of the ugly parasites; but at the same time drawn towards Samson out of sympathy for her beloved dog. The tension between the two emotions was palpable. She panicked. She did all the wrong things and did them quickly.

Ticks, ordinary ticks, are small arachnids that evolved many millions of years ago, in the Cretaceous period, and have survived those millions of years by feeding on the blood of animals. So-called hard ticks, which the ones on Samson were, have what looks like a pointed-shaped head at the front of their bodies; but it is not a head – it contains neither brains nor eyes – it is more a beak-like structure with mouthparts perfectly developed for their function of piercing skin and sucking blood. These mouthparts work to extract blood by cutting a hole in the host's skin into which is inserted a calcified harpoon-like structure called a hypostome. This has barbed edges and anchors the tick firmly in place whilst it sucks blood. The tick also excretes an anticoagulant into its host to prevent its blood from clotting. Ticks can carry disease through a variety of pathogens – whether bacteria, virus or protozoa – and a single tick can harbour more than one type of pathogen. As a consequence of all this, ticks need to be removed with every care. If you squeeze the tick to remove it, the body will separate from the 'head', leaving the head imbedded in the skin. If you remove a tick with your fingernails, you risk infection entering through any breaks in your skin which there might be close to or under the end of your fingernail.

If you crush the tick's body, it may cause it to regurgitate its infected stomach contents into the bite wound of its host. If you crush an engorged tick it will burst and spatter potentially infected blood on you.

Rachel, in her panic, attempted to remove as many of the ticks that infested Samson's face and ears as she could, brushing them away with her fingers. The blood-filled bodies of engorged ticks came away, leaving their heads embedded in Samson's face and ears. Unattached engorged tick bodies burst like overripe berries, covering Rachel's hands in Samson's blood. Crushed ticks regurgitated their infected stomach contents back into the bite wounds in Samson's body through which the feast had originally been sucked. Live ticks that had yet to attach themselves to Samson and were wandering through his fur, still seeking out places like the inside of his ears and around his eyes where the skin was at its thinnest, moved about – almost as if in panic at the carnage that was being inflicted on their brethren. At least one bit Rachel and attached itself to her skin.

How could this have happened? How could these ticks have filled Samson's face and ears so quickly? How could they have gorged themselves so quickly? Thoughts raced through Rachel's head as she screamed and Samson howled. How could it be? *How could it be?* HOW COULD IT BE? Ordinary dog ticks couldn't do this so quickly.

It happened these weren't entirely ordinary ticks.

VI

The scalpel was steady in Dennis's hands. He'd done this many times, after all. He drew the sharp blade across the skin on a part of his forearm and let the blood drip into a petri dish that had been positioned to collect it. It was feeding time for his little zoo again.

In some ways, it was a major lack of imagination or foresight on the part of schools and academia that had let Dennis down. He truly possessed in his own small way a genius that they failed to nurture or acknowledge. In another universe, his natural gift for understanding the natural world without formal education and his dedication might have made him a celebrated biologist, an outstanding researcher or even a breeder of prize livestock. But worthwhile scientific careers and breeding useful animals were the fortune of others. Dennis bred ticks, selecting as breeding stock only the largest and hardiest specimens, those that fed the fastest and moved the quickest. Because of the short life cycle of the tick, giant strides were possible in a space of time that breeders of pedigree dogs or thoroughbred racehorses could only dream of; and Dennis had been doing this for years. As the results improved and improved, Dennis's dedication only grew and his other interests and ambitions fell away. Amongst other things, and although like aging the process was imperceptible day by day, Dennis ultimately gave up on any hopes of female companionship. There was no moment of epiphany, just a subliminal acceptance of Einstein's definition of madness; unconsciously Dennis came to end his endeavours in trying to attract women. He had never been very successful at doing so, and the few relationships he had managed to have had all ended badly. They would lose whatever interest they had in him quickly; someone taller, more successful or better looking would turn their heads – and Dennis's heart would break. The results were the same every time: crushing. So, like the sane scientist who ultimately gives up repeating the same experiment and expecting to get a different result, Dennis gave up on relationships. It wasn't a giving up on life, though. After all, Dennis had something a little bit more special than being married with children or being in a relationship; he had a vat full of the strongest, fastest, hardiest and biggest ticks mankind had ever known.

VII

Five weeks after the ticks incident, Rachel sat in her doctors' surgery waiting to be called in for her appointment. The best way to get a doctor's appointment at the medical centre local to her and Thomas was to ring up on the day. If you did so early enough, you'd normally manage to get one, but the disadvantage with this was that you had to take pot luck as to which doctor you got to see. Rachel had hoped for an appointment with the female doctor who always shook her patients' hands when she greeted them, and who always wore a dress, and who always ran late with her appointments as she genuinely seemed to care about listening to her patients – what was her name? Instead, Rachel's appointment was with Dr Metcalf, who it seemed was more interested in his imminent retirement than he was his patients. He let Rachel talk herself out about how bad she felt, how her muscles ached, how her neck always seemed to be stiff, how she had problems remembering things properly and how low she was feeling after she had lost her dog Samson; before he interjected with any questions. She left with a prescription for an increased dose of the anti-depressant Sertraline and without feeling she'd been listened to at all.

Inside Rachel's body the infection the extraordinary ticks had blessed her with carried on its inexorable progress deeper into her brain.

Rachel took the increased dose of Sertraline as directed, but it seemed to do little to lighten her mood, and just made her mouth feel increasingly dry and sounded the death knell for what little interest she had left in sex after her world had felt like it had collapsed when Samson had had to be put down. Thomas, of course, noticed the inexorable decline in his wife's mood. After all, he loved her greatly and she had been his soul-mate of the past eight years. He tried to suggest evenings out. A meal out with a couple who were old friends of theirs was arranged and cancelled as Rachel told him she just couldn't face it. A meal out for just to two of them at their town's most expensive restaurant was booked and similarly cancelled; it was even easier for Rachel to turn that evening out down, as it only involved the two of them and letting one person down. Thomas even suggested they bought a new puppy as a way to help ease his wife's malaise. He tried to show her the puppies that were listed online – German Shepherds as they called them these days, but they would always be Alsatians to him. There were some beautiful dogs for sale, from puppies cute as buttons that wouldn't be ready to leave for weeks to handsome dogs in the latter months of their first year ready to leave for a new home as soon as possible. Money wasn't a problem for them to buy one. They could pick it up right away if they chose one that was old enough. But as he tried to show Rachel some of the dogs' pictures he'd found, she slapped the laptop out of his hands so it crashed to the floor.

Rachel's mood was little better at work; although she managed to keep outbursts like the laptop incident reserved for her nearest and dearest. She enjoyed a fairly senior position, so there was no one watching over her shoulder to notice that she spent more time staring into space than she did actually working at her computer. There was no clocking in or out system as such at her workplace. Maybe someone looked at the records that the electronic access system undoubtedly produced as employees let themselves in and out, but she doubted it. In any event, she found it easy to arrive at work progressively later, leave progressively earlier and take longer lunch breaks without anyone commenting, at least to her face. Maybe her line manager would pick her up on the dwindling time she spent actually working eventually, but even then the initial threat to Rachel would just be an uncomfortable chat rather than anything more serious. Rachel's previous achievements and good reputation at work would hold her in good stead for a while. She'd simply lost interest in her job. She took on less projects and pretended to be busy when she wasn't. She took occasional sick days when even the effort of pretending to be interested was too much.

One day about a year after the day of the ticks, Rachel took a sick day and never returned to work, ever. Her sickness was by now all too real, and her physical health as well as her mental health had been destroyed.

By this stage, Thomas had long ago given up trying to take his wife out of herself with invitations that were always turned down, or more latterly that were met with outright hostility. Rachel's friends had faced the same deteriorating progression of responses to their concern, invitations and offers of help. They too asked less and less, and then drifted away. Thomas, himself, had nowhere to drift away to as such. He still lived with Rachel, still slept in the same bed as Rachel; but, without perhaps fully realising it himself, he began to put less effort in to trying to communicate with his wife. He gave up suggesting things they could do together. He gave up trying to persuade her to go back to the doctors. He spent less time with her. He found other things to do that were less frustrating, more enjoyable. Perhaps like Dennis before him in a different set of circumstances, Thomas subconsciously gave in to the logic of Einstein's definition of madness, whether or not there could really have been an alternative choice, an alternative pattern of behaviour.

In years to come he would curse himself every day for not having tried harder and for not having realised the seriousness of the situation.

VIII

Dennis couldn't resist.

On seeing Thomas, he dived out the way into the toilet for the disabled that happened to be near him in the hospital corridor. Once inside the door, he thrust his right hand down the front of his trousers and rubbed it around his sweaty genitals. Removing his hand, he gave it a quick sniff, as if to prove to himself that he had done what he had just done. It had a feint, musky smell of old urine and sweat that he found strangely pleasing. He dived back out into the corridor and chased after Thomas, approaching him.

'I'm so sorry,' he said as his thrust his right hand forward for Thomas to shake. Unwittingly Thomas shook it.

'Who ... What ...?' Thomas managed to get out, the unspoken remainder of the questions being obvious, *who was this odd little man? what did he want?*

'I so sorry. I knew Rachel, you see. We were girlfriend and boyfriend before you met her.' This was a lie or at best a gross exaggeration. Rachel and Dennis had been out on one date where the conversation had flowed like tarmac that had already set. It had taken all Dennis's courage to call Rachel the following day to ask for a second date, but she had quickly rebutted him explaining that if he hadn't noticed they had hardly got on very well and that, no, she would not have any interest in seeing him again. To Rachel, Dennis had just been one of the frogs along the way, before she met her prince, Thomas. If you had have shown her a photo of Dennis in the hours before she died, she would have been hard-pressed to remember him at all. Why would she? It had been one lousy date a decade earlier where there may have been a kiss and some stilted conversation, but nothing else happened. To Dennis, Rachel had been his world at that point, the person that dominated his thoughts from morning to night and on into his dreams. He'd admired her from afar for months beforehand, and when she agreed to a date with him it felt like all his dreams had just come true. She seemed to him then so perfect, so right for him; and for the rest of his life Rachel came to define for him the ideal, the essence, of what an attractive woman was. All other women could be judged in terms of the traits they shared with Rachel and how much they looked like Rachel. Rachel was petite and thin. So, petite and thin was part of how Dennis came to define attractiveness to himself. Rachel wore her brown her long and swept back from her face in style that almost belonged to a different time, but suited her tremendously. Dennis looked for that hairstyle in other women.

'Really?' Thomas was a little taken aback by this stranger's statement, and certainly didn't want to have anything further to do with him.

'Yes, I'm Dennis, Dennis Stevens.'

'She never mentioned you. Look, I'm not in the mood

for conversation right now. My wife's *just died*. Just leave me alone, eh?'

'Yes, had things been different I might have married her, you know?'

'Look,' said Thomas, losing his temper easily at this man, 'just *fuck off* and leave me alone.' With that, he pushed past Dennis and walked briskly away from him.

IX

Back at home, Dennis quickly found his peace of mind deteriorating. He tried to eat, but found he had to force the food down against no appetite for it at all. It wasn't supposed to be like this. He hadn't meant Rachel to die. How could he have even imagined that consequence. It was surely a freak medical event. They would write textbooks about her case in years to come. He told himself he wasn't evil. He hadn't wanted this to happen. Maybe if it had been Thomas that had died. Yes, he could have delighted in an unintended consequence like that. He could imagine himself celebrating that with a bottle of a sweet, dry Champagne; the taste of revenge would have been at least as sweet as the drink. As it was, nothing felt sweet and he found himself drinking whatever alcohol he could find in the kitchen cupboard where he kept the likes of a bottle of cheap wine and a half empty bottle of gin, just to try and blot out the emotions that where making his every conscious moment one he would rather be without. He paced his tiny home, going from room to room as if that minor change of environment would make any difference to his mood, to his feelings of distress and guilt. And as he paced the rooms, he drank. He drank till his head became a fuzz, till he felt dizzy and nauseous, and till his eyes refused to focus properly.

No, it hadn't meant to be like this. A little bit of minor revenge against the world that constantly rejected him, against womankind that constantly treated him with disdain, and in particular against the woman he had wanted most in the world and who had cruelly spurned him – that was all he had wanted. He had so enjoyed the taste of revenge he had experienced with that first dog years ago. He had been waiting outside Rachel and her stupid husband's house. Well, waiting a little way down the street, so as not to be obvious. Sat in his car, just waiting for a sight of Rachel that he could enjoy. He had no photographs of her then and regularly made sure he found a way to keep sight of her, lest the picture he carried of her in his mind would start to fade. And then, he saw the dog bound from the garden. It looked like a younger, smaller version of the Alsatian his parents had had and that he hated so. What an opportunity. Acting on a decision that took him only seconds to make, he started his car and gunned it at the dog. The manoeuvre was perfect. He hit the dog square on and its lifeless body hit the ground with a minimum of fuss and noise. He was frightened the incident would have attracted the attention of, if not Rachel or her husband, one of their neighbours; but as it was, nobody came out from their house, no curtains even twitched. He prodded the body with his foot to make sure it was dead, then – steeling himself to do this, as he hated touching dogs at the best of times – he picked up the corpse and, again praying he wouldn't be seen, placed the lifeless dog on Rachel's doorstep. He drove home that day with a broad smile on his face.

Years later, his actions had been ones that were planned in advance. He knew Rachel's movements well. He knew more or less the time she and her husband could be found walking their dog in the woods. He practised dry-runs, watching Rachel, husband and dog from behind the cover of trees, never once being spotted. Then when he felt the time was right he acted, tempting the dog away from its owners with a piece of fresh meat and introducing the animal to a quantity of his genetically-superior ticks, the experience feeling all the more sweet because the dog bore a striking resemblance to the hated dog his parents kept.

Too dizzy and vision too blurred for it to be comfortable to do anything other than stop moving, Dennis sat on the floor of his hobby room staring at the vat full of his best ticks. The thoughts raced in his head, burning through his peace of mind like a forest fire. This was horrible, like being in love with someone who hated you, all bitter and no sweet. Like being dumped, only worse. He kicked out with his foot in anger, before falling into drunken unconsciousness.

The vat of ticks collapsed to the floor in a mass of living beings and broken glass. The ticks spread out on the floor like a living carpet. They crawled all over Dennis's body, heading with speed and alacrity for the parts where the skin was the thinnest and unobstructed by clothing. Within hours, Dennis's whole head was a mass of bulbous engorged berries that were the bodies of the ticks impaled in his skin and that were feeding on his blood. It would be a slow, painful death.

THE TALE OF SAMUEL AND GORDON

Keith Trezise

I

Samuel and Gordon had always been friends. At school they did everything together. If either one got top marks at maths, the other would achieve the second highest mark. They both played rugby for the school and were each made captain for alternate seasons. Samuel excelled at cricket, whilst Gordon played wonderful tennis. They were also joint holders of the 'Sportsman of the Year' trophy. They were not insufferable swots, however, and neither of them showed off about their prowess on the sports field.

Their tastes were quite alike. They both enjoyed sausages and mash, the FA Cup, big hairy spiders, marbles, choc-ices, pulling girls' hair, playing soldiers and rice pudding. The only difference was that whereas Samuel was lucky, Gordon was not.

Samuel lived happily with his mother and father and sister and Jacob, the Labrador. Gordon's father had left home and his brother, Joe, was killed by a hit-and-run driver, and his mother was crippled with arthritis. Samuel was a handsome boy with fair, wavy hair and deep blue eyes. Gordon wore thick glasses over his brown eyes, and his dark hair was straight and always greasy. The two boys loved to laugh – but Samuel's laughter always seemed much brighter and more spontaneous than Gordon's.

When they left school, Samuel went to university, but Gordon had to find work so that he could support his invalid mother. The two friends kept in touch for a while, but soon the letters became less frequent and the reunions dwindled until, finally, they saw nothing of one another.

Gordon worked harder and harder. His mother's condition continued to deteriorate and the treatment became more and more expensive. Before long it became obvious that she was going to die. Gordon wrote to his father and begged him to come home, but the letter was returned unopened and marked 'Gone away'.

That night, Gordon's mother called to him. Her voice was very faint because she was so weak, and Gordon had to put his ear very close to her mouth so that he could hear her speak.

'Gordon,' she said, 'you are a good boy. You have worked hard and looked after your mother very well. But now I have to leave you. First, I must tell you about the things you must do when I die.'

'No, Mother!' Gordon cried. 'You must not talk that way.'

'You have only yourself to look after now,' she continued, 'and you must make something of yourself. Promise me that you will.' She summoned all her strength to gently squeeze his hand.

A tear rolled down Gordon's cheek as he said, 'I promise, Mother.'

'I believe you, my son,' she said. And then she died.

II

Just after the funeral, Samuel arrived back in town. He had been newly appointed as a director of the company that employed Gordon. One day, Samuel bumped into Gordon on the shop floor, but when Gordon tried to greet his old friend, Samuel simply turned his back on him and went about his business. The very next day, Gordon lost his job.

Times were hard and, although the government spoke of unprecedented economic growth, it was not easy for Gordon to find work. After searching in vain for many weeks, Gordon decided to call on Samuel and, if necessary, beg him to give him his old job back. Samuel refused to see him.

Soon, Gordon became desperately poor and was unable to pay the rent on his apartment. After several weeks, he received a letter demanding that he settled the arrears on his rent or be faced with eviction. It was with some surprise that Gordon noticed Samuel's name amongst the directors of the company that owned the apartment building. He thought that if he could speak to Samuel, they might be able to come to some arrangement with the rent and he might also persuade Samuel to give him his job back. Again Samuel would not see him, and the following week the bailiffs came and made him leave his home.

Gordon was at an all-time low. He had no money, no job and no home. He was forced to walk the streets begging for crusts. He had to sleep in shop doorways, or subways or any nook or cranny that might offer shelter from the elements. People were unkind to him. They would throw stones or shout abuse, for no other reason than it made them feel good.

Somehow, perhaps by chance, Gordon found a job as a

caretaker of a block of flats. The pay was not fantastic, but he was given an apartment rent free and things started to get better. Especially as, at nearly the same time he landed the job, he met a wonderful girl called Penelope and fell instantly in love with her. Each day, as soon as Gordon finished work, he would call on Penelope and they would hold hands and say silly things to one another. For the first time in years, Gordon was starting to feel happy. He would say to Penelope, 'I love you more than sixpence.' And she would blush and rest her head on his shoulder and say, 'When will we be married?' and Gordon would say, 'When things get better.'

After a few months, Gordon did not call on Penelope quite so often, because she would say that she had to wash her hair or that she was going out with a girlfriend. Finally Penelope told Gordon the truth – that she did not love him anymore and that she was seeing another man. Gordon knew that the other man was Samuel, even before Penelope told him. Not long after losing Penelope, Gordon also lost his job and apartment, because of a redevelopment involving one of Samuel's companies.

It seemed that the more Samuel prospered, the more Gordon suffered. Gordon started to feel hatred for his former friend, and when he fell asleep at night he would dream that he was an insect and Samuel kept crushing him underfoot.

The time soon came when Gordon was so poor and despondent that he decided he no longer wanted to live. He walked a few miles to the middle of a high bridge that spanned a very fast flowing river and made his mind up to throw himself into the water and die.

He would have done it too – if the man had not stopped him.

III

The man appeared as if from nowhere, and he told Gordon that he was being extremely stupid – wanting to die. Not knowing what there was left to live for, Gordon asked, 'What good is life to me?'

The man laughed loud and long and, as he did so, a strange wind sprang up, ripping the leaves from the trees. Gordon was frightened.

'What good is life to me?' the man mocked. 'What good is death? Ha! Ha! I have the power to give you the very best of both!' The wind died down as suddenly as it started.

'I do not understand,' said Gordon quite truthfully.

'I don't suppose you do!' snarled the man. 'But I will explain.' At this point the man paused as if to provide his next statement with the full theatrical effect that he felt it deserved. 'Do you believe in ghosts?'

'No,' said Gordon, 'it's all idiotic nonsense.'

'Don't be so quick to deny it!' There seemed to be a little anger in the man's voice. 'You ought to believe in them because they are real. They do exist. They are as real as you or I. In fact, you and I are ghosts.'

'What are you talking about?'

'You're a ghost – a spirit.'

'I'm dead?'

'No. You are not dead. But your life-force is your spirit, and your spirit is your ghost, and so that ghost is you. This body of yours is merely a vehicle for your spirit. It serves to transport your spirit within this lifetime. Your spirit may inhabit many bodies over many lifetimes, but there is always the same problem. Whilst in your body, your spirit is trapped within its mortal limitations. But I can show you how to break free of the chains with which your body shackles your spirit. I can show you how to release the ghost within.'

Gordon said, 'I do not know if I want to.'

'Come now!' the man roared. 'You made a promise to your mother. You promised that you would make something of yourself. Do you want to fail her?'

'Of course not,' Gordon said. His eyes filled with tears at the thought of his poor dead mother.

'Then it is agreed. I will give you the gift you need.'

'And what do you want in return?' asked Gordon.

'Nothing,' said the man, 'except one tiny drop of your blood.' And the man pricked Gordon's hand so that a single drop of blood fell to the ground. The man started walking away.

'But what about the gift?' Gordon shouted at the retreating figure.

'You must turn to your dreams tonight,' the man replied and, as he walked away, Gordon noticed that the sun was playing tricks with the man's shadow. It was not the shadow of a man, but that of some kind of horned animal. A goat, perhaps, walking upright on its two hind legs. A trick of the sunlight.

IV

That night, Gordon decided to sleep by the river inside a large hollow tree that would protect him from the cold wind. He rolled into a ball, covering himself in fallen leaves. As he lay there waiting for slumber, he could hear the gurgling water protesting as it hurried towards the ocean many miles away. He heard the screech of an owl as it conducted its nightly patrol in search of prey, and then he slept.

He dreamed, at first, that he was a fly. He sensed the freedom of being able to go wherever he pleased. It was an exhilarating feeling. He climbed up sheer walls and climbed over ceilings. He flew into larders and feasted on gorgonzola cheese and sugar. He watched the world with a myriad of eyes and rejoiced in his freedom. He crawled into an open cupboard where there was an enormous piece of cake and he started to gorge himself with the tasty treat. Soon, he had eaten so much food that he was too heavy and could no longer fly. Then he found that he could not walk either. His six legs were stuck fast. His heart pounded fiercely when he realised that he was trapped in a spider's web. His whole body shook with fear as he saw the spider creeping towards him, its huge jaws moving to and fro in anticipation of the meal to come. Gordon watched transfixed as the spider's face began a horrible metamorphosis. Instead of a hungry spider bearing down on him, he saw a hungry Samuel preparing to devour him. Samuel – the spider – opened its mouth and the jaws stretched wider as they closed in on Gordon. Just as the huge mouth was about to engulf him, Gordon awoke from his dream. Although the night air was cold, he was sweating. He thought about this terrible dream for a while, but decided that it did not contain the secret of the man's gift, and so he settled back down and was soon asleep again.

V

In his second dream Gordon was a mouse. He lived in a very large house where the owners were lazy and rich and had no cat. The owners would never clear away after their meals and would fall asleep at the table. They never saw

Gordon the mouse as he climbed up onto the table and ate the remains from their dinner plates. Gordon would climb onto the fruit bowl and take just one bite out of every piece of fruit. Then he would wash down his feast with some wine from an upset wineglass and, when he had eaten and drunk all that he could, he would go back to his hole and sleep until the next mealtime. He enjoyed the freedom of the whole house and ate and drank as heartily as the owners did.

One day he climbed up onto the table to have his dinner as usual, but the mistress of the house woke up before he had finished, and when she saw him she let out a terrible shriek. Gordon scampered back to his hole in an awful fright. After a while, he heard something being pushed up against the entrance to his home. He went to investigate and, to his surprise, found that it was an enormous piece of gorgonzola cheese. It seemed the owners were not afraid of him after all and they wanted to feed him and look after him. The cheese smelled delicious and, as he had not finished his meal, he decided to eat it. But no sooner had he sniffed at the gorgonzola than a huge metal bar slammed down on him, shaving off one of his whiskers – he had seen the trap just in time. He was a very lucky mouse to still be alive as he scampered further into his hole. The owners were trying to kill him, and he must always be on his guard in the future whenever he went near any food.

The owners soon grew tired of trying to catch Gordon in their mousetraps and so they bought a cat. They called it Penelope and it was very hungry for mice. Gordon knew that he could no longer live in the house, and so he left and went into the garden. It was a dark night and he was very frightened as he scurried across the lawn.

'Look out!' warned a large bullfrog, and Gordon just

managed to dive for cover as a huge owl swooped down. Luckily the owl missed him, and Gordon ran on and on as fast as he could into the night. He ran in terror across a busy road where he nearly met his death in the heavy flow of traffic. He ran and ran until it was morning, too tired to carry on, but too frightened to stop. Finally he had to rest, so he dropped to the ground quite exhausted.

He gasped to catch his breath and there, quite close by, he saw an eye staring at him.

Gordon was very scared, but he was far too tired to be able to run away. The eye moved closer and he could see that it belonged to a snake. He was still too tired to run as the snake slithered towards him at a frightening speed, and as the snake's jaw unhinged to swallow him whole he saw that it had Samuel's face.

Gordon woke up in another sweat and knew that this was not the dream that he was waiting for either. By the light of the moon he saw an owl swoop down and grab a mouse in its talons and fly off with the poor creature squealing in terror.

VI

In his third dream Gordon was a young boy again. He was sitting down to dinner with his mother and father and brother Joe. They were eating a Christmas dinner and a huge log fire was blazing in the hearth.

'Gordon,' his father said, 'why are you so sad?'

'Because you ran away, Father,' he replied. 'Why did you leave my mother to care for Joe and me on her own?'

'That is easy to answer, my son. Samuel told me that I must go. He told me to stop loving you all.' And then Gordon's father vanished, leaving behind a pile of ashes on the chair where he had been sitting.

'Gordon,' his brother Joe said, 'why are you so sad?'

'Because you are dead, my dear brother,' he replied. 'Why did you have to die so young, leaving our mother with a broken heart?'

'That is easy to answer, my brother. Samuel caused my death and he will cause yours too, no doubt.' And, so saying, Joe vanished, leaving behind a pile of black rose petals on the chair where he had been sitting.

'Gordon,' his mother said (her voice was so weak that he had to put his ear close to her mouth to hear her words), 'why are you so sad?'

'Because you are dead too, my beloved mother. Why could I not have earned more money to pay for better treatment?'

'That is easy to answer, my son. Samuel would not allow it. He hates you and wants to bring you nothing but misery.' Then she vanished, leaving behind a pile of dried leaves on the chair where she had been sitting.

Gordon buried his face in his hands and wept. The three people he loved most had all been destroyed by Samuel.

'Do not cry, Gordon,' said the man. 'I have come to give you the gift I spoke of.'

Gordon looked up and saw the man standing by the fire. 'What do I have to do?' he asked.

The man gave Gordon a leather pouch and said, 'Fill this with the ashes, black rose petals and dried leaves that your loved ones left behind.'

Gordon did as he was told.

'Now, hold out your hand,' the man added.

Gordon did so and the man pricked his hand so that a single drop of blood fell to the ground.

The man said, 'Now you must swear allegiance to me and I will grant you the gift of being able to free your spirit

from the confines of your body. You will be able to release
the ghost within. Do you swear allegiance?'

When Gordon awoke, the sun was high in the sky and
the birds were singing a most glorious song in the trees. He
felt rejuvenated and knew that things were going to get
better. As he stood up to stretch the sleep from his body,
something fell from his lap. He bent down and picked up
the leather pouch from where it had fallen. He could not
believe that it was really there. When he opened it, he
found that it contained a mixture of ashes, black rose petals
and dried leaves. It was really true. The man had given him
the gift to release the ghost within. Gordon put the leather
pouch in his pocket ready for the journey to town. As he
left the hollow tree, he passed the place where the drop of
blood had fallen from his hand to the ground. All around
the place where it had fallen the grass was burned away and
the ground was full of dead worms. Gordon felt a shiver
run down his spine as he took the road that led back
towards the town.

VII

As Gordon walked into town he passed a shop which had a
notice in the window. The notice read 'WANTED:
ASSISTANT – APPLY WITHIN'. Gordon went into the
shop and the shopkeeper gave him the job right there and
then. Gordon knew that his luck had changed for the
better. He worked well and the shopkeeper let him live in a
spare room above the shop.

When night fell Gordon went up to his room and lay on
his bed. He took the leather pouch out of his pocket and
held it tightly in his hand. 'Now, my spirit,' he said, 'I set
you free.' He closed his eyes and waited – but nothing

happened. He had been tricked. He was unable to release the ghost within. He sat up on the edge of the bed and opened up the pouch. It was full of ashes, black rose petals and dried leaves. It was truly amazing, the way in which he had come by this trinket, but it was useless for the purpose it was given to him.

Gordon was about to toss the leather pouch to one side when he noticed something written on the outside of it. It was a strange-looking word written in dried blood. He lay back down on the bed again and studied the strange word. He tried to say it out aloud, but it was an extremely difficult word to pronounce.

After a little practice, however, he managed to say it without too much trouble and, when he was confident that he had mastered it, he closed his eyes and said it out aloud and added, 'Set my spirit free.'

Gordon's eyes became very heavy, and it felt as if he was falling into a very deep sleep. His arm and leg muscles tensed slightly before relaxing completely, and soon he could not feel his body at all.

Gordon sensed that, at last, he was free from the confines of his body, but was not really sure what to do next. He thought about it for a while and decided that he would like to look down on his body from above. No sooner had this entered his thoughts than he felt himself rising up into the air. He looked around and saw that he was floating just below the ceiling of his room. He looked down and saw his body on the bed, lying in a peaceful slumber. On seeing his own body lying there seemingly lifeless, he was filled with tremendous apprehension. He wanted his spirit to rejoin his body. Almost at once, he felt himself drifting down and entering his body again. He said the strange word and added, 'Rejoin my body and spirit!'

After a short while he could feel his arms and legs again, and was soon awake. Gordon's pulse raced. He was both frightened and excited by his new power. All he had to do now was work out how to use that power to his advantage. It would take time, but eventually he would work it out. Before long Gordon fell asleep.

VIII

That night Gordon dreamed that he was a bird flying freely through the sky, catching insects in his beak. As he soared through the clouds, he looked down and saw the whole world at his feet. He was flying so high that he could see the roundness of the Earth. It was as if he was only a wing tip away from the sun.

Gordon flew higher and higher, and was soon weaving in and out of the stars until he finally came to rest on the topmost branch of a tall silver tree on the bright side of the moon. He had transformed into a splendid red and gold eagle, and the surface of the moon below him was made of gorgonzola cheese. The moon was overrun with enormous mice, all hungry for the gorgonzola cheese. Gordon knew it would be easy to catch these slow, overweight mice and have a feast. He watched them for a while from his perch in the tall silver tree towering over the moon's surface. He saw how they were all so fat from eating gorgonzola cheese that they could not run very fast at all. Easy pickings. He stretched out his gigantic wings and swooped down to pick several mice up in his powerful claws. As he carried them back to his perch, he noticed that their faces were all the same – they all looked like Samuel. He devoured them all with one swallow.

IX

In the morning Gordon awoke refreshed. He had slept well and went about his work in a cheerful manner. He could not remember the last time that he had felt so happy.

He pondered all day over his wonderful gift and how he might be able to use it to his advantage, so much so that he did not work as well as he should have and the shopkeeper became angry.

'I do not pay you to sit there and daydream!' the shopkeeper cried. Gordon apologised and worked harder than ever. When his work for the day had finished, Gordon ran up to his room and quickly took the leather pouch from his pocket and gazed at it. His heart began to pound at the thought of setting his spirit free again. He lay down on his bed and said the strange word and added, 'Set my spirit free!'

This time when his spirit floated free from his body he drifted up through the roof of the shop and up into the night sky. He did not feel the coldness of the air, only his freedom. He felt like the bird in his dream as he looked down on the world below, and almost considered flying to the moon. Just then a light went on in the backroom of the shop, and he decided to go and investigate. His spirit drifted down into the room and he saw the shopkeeper doing his accounts. The shopkeeper was a very rich man indeed. Gordon wondered how he could make the shopkeeper's wealth his own. Surely with that much money he could make something of himself and fulfil his promise to his mother. And maybe get back at Samuel at the same time. He had seen enough for one night and decided to return to his body. That night, Gordon dreamed that the shopkeeper died and left his entire estate to him in his will.

The dream of the shopkeeper's death played on Gordon's mind until it became an obsession. It was the ideal way to get hold of his fortune. He worked harder and harder in the shop, and worked on befriending the shopkeeper and, eventually, the shopkeeper came to regard Gordon as though he were his own son. The shopkeeper made a will bequeathing his entire estate to Gordon. The plan had taken quite some time to put into place, and Gordon used that time to practice his power and became stronger. All that was left to do was for Gordon to arrange for the shopkeeper to die.

X

One evening Gordon went into the town for a drink, and when it was time for the inn to close he started arguing with the landlord.

'You cannot close yet,' Gordon shouted. 'I have not finished.'

The landlord threatened to call the police if Gordon did not leave, but Gordon said, 'I will not leave yet, because I have not finished.'

So the landlord did call the police, and Gordon was arrested and put into a cell for the night. This was exactly what he wanted. He hadn't wanted to be parted from his leather pouch, though, and had reasoned quite correctly that the police might want to remove a suspicious-looking herbal package from him before locking him up. But he had also reasoned correctly that the police were unlikely to subject him to an internal body search simply for being drunk and being obstreperous. He had therefore literally taken the pains to secrete the leather pouch within his intimate person with the aid of a prophylactic sheath and some Vaseline.

When he was quite alone in the cell, Gordon lay down on the bunk and closed his eyes and said the strange word and set his spirit free.

Higher and higher he floated until he rose far above the church steeple. He could see the whole town beneath him. He could see the school where he had first met Samuel. He could see the apartment block where he and his family had lived. He could see the block of flats where his caretaker's apartment had once been. He could see the factory where he had worked until Samuel had thrown him out. More importantly, he could see the shop where he worked and lived.

Gordon floated across the town until he was above the shop and then, like the eagle of his dream, he swooped down into the shopkeeper's bedroom. All that was left to do was to press the pillow against the shopkeeper's face until he was quite dead.

However, when Gordon reached for the pillow he found that he could not pick it up. His hands passed right through it. He tried once more, but again he could not grasp the pillow.

'You can do it, Gordon,' the man's voice said. 'Concentrate. Will yourself to do it. You have the power.'

'I can do it,' Gordon said as he reached for the pillow again. This time he could actually feel the pillow with his ghostly hands, and he knew his plan was going to work. He placed the pillow across the shopkeeper's face and pressed down firmly. The sleeping figure did not even struggle.

Suddenly, Gordon heard a sickening, piercing, high-pitched scream as the shopkeeper's spirit leaped from its body with a grotesquely contorted face filled with agony and terror. The spirit moved menacingly towards Gordon, but some unknown force was pulling it back until it faded, screaming, into nothing. The shopkeeper was dead and, with the knowledge of the wealth to come, Gordon guided his spirit back into his body. Next – it would be Samuel's turn.

XI

Although Gordon was quite rich, nothing could rid him of his desire for terrible revenge against Samuel. Samuel who used to be his dearest friend was now his bitterest enemy. It was plain to see that Samuel was evil incarnate and had to be destroyed. Was it not Samuel who destroyed Gordon's family? Was it not Samuel who took Gordon's job and home away? Was it not Samuel who stole Penelope away and nearly caused Gordon to take his own life? Well, now it was Samuel's turn to suffer. These were the thoughts that occupied Gordon's mind day and night until, finally, he knew that the time had come to kill his one-time friend.

Gordon called his doctor and complained of terrible stomach pains. The doctor arrived and gave Gordon a very thorough examination, but could find nothing wrong. When Gordon insisted that he was in terrible pain, the doctor admitted him to hospital for observation. Gordon's plan was running like clockwork. This spell in hospital would provide the perfect alibi for Gordon on the night of Samuel's murder. He would again be above suspicion.

XII

A nurse came and gave Gordon some tablets to ease his 'pain' and help him to sleep, but when Gordon put them into his mouth, he hid them under his tongue and did not swallow them. He pretended to be asleep and, when the nurse had gone away, he took the tablets out and threw them away.

The other patients were very restless and moaned in pain for a long time, but eventually they all fell asleep. Gordon slipped out of bed and checked every patient, and when he was satisfied that they were all asleep he climbed back in his own bed, closed his eyes and said the strange word. In no time at all his spirit was floating free. He drifted through the large hospital, looking down on all the captive spirits inside their pain-ridden bodies, and he laughed a long laugh of joy at his own perfect freedom.

Gordon's spirit drifted higher and higher. Through the hospital roof he rose, up into the clouds. He looked down on the town below, and was filled with an immense feeling of power.

'Ha! Ha!' he laughed. 'All you poor wretches below! You are mine to do with as I please! I have the power of life and death over you all! I have the power of a God!' He laughed again. He laughed loud and long, and a wind suddenly sprang up which ripped the leaves from the trees. He flew across the whole town, laughing maniacally as he went, and the wind he had conjured laid all the trees bare. Dogs howled at the moonless sky and the creatures of the night hid in fear.

By the time he had reached Samuel's house, his faithful wind had worked up into such a frenzy that it tore up trees in its path. Storm clouds gathered overhead, and bolts of lightning flashed to the ground causing a great deal of damage. Gordon could feel a surge of power every time a lightning bolt flashed through the sky. The dark storm clouds bubbled and boiled and their underbellies changed colour incessantly, displaying every hue imaginable. The lightning bolts no longer crashed to the ground, but sent their charges directly towards Gordon's spirit, strengthening it for the task ahead. Gordon raised his hands and streams of pure electricity pulsed from his fingertips. He pointed his forefinger at a car in the street and it disintegrated with a flash of blinding light as the energy from Gordon hit its mark.

Now that Gordon was the storm, the redundant clouds grouped together and, as Gordon summoned them to him, they transformed into a host of demons from the depths of hell and they bowed down before Gordon's spirit and paid homage to him. There were hundreds of bestial forms waiting to do his bidding. Gordon pointed to Samuel's house and cried, 'We must destroy that man!'

The thunderstorm emanating from Gordon's spirit grew in intensity, and the air was filled with demonic laughter. Two of the demons, with twisted and tormented faces, descended on the house and carried Samuel aloft to Gordon. Samuel awoke from his sleep and saw the terrible sight and thought that he was having a nightmare – unfortunately for him, he was not. The host of demons bore down on him at Gordon's command. They were all hungry for the taste of human flesh. Samuel's screams filled the night sky.

Horrid, horny hands tore at Samuel's flesh until it hung from his body in ghastly ribbons and distorted, fiendish faces feasted furiously on him. Samuel shrieked as ghastly, gangrenous ghouls grabbed his arms and legs and tore them from his body before devouring them whole. All the time Samuel wailed in agony and terror. All the time the demonic laughter grew louder.

Finally, Gordon thrust his hand deep into Samuel's chest and tore out his living heart. The demons begged him for the tasty morsel, but Gordon denied them all as he opened his mouth and swallowed it whole. Then Samuel was dead. The hordes from hell departed, and Gordon's spirit made its triumphant way back to the hospital. The taste of revenge was sweet in Gordon's mouth and he was happy.

Gordon floated back down to his hospital bed and said the strange word – but nothing happened. He could not re-enter his body because it was no longer there. He began to feel afraid. Where would his body be? He searched all over the hospital, but was unable to find it anywhere. There was but one place left to look and Gordon was afraid that he would find his body there. It was the mortuary.

XIII

Gordon floated down through the ceiling of the mortuary and there he saw his body. He was not alone, for there beside him floated the spirit of a beautiful young woman.

'Are we dead?' she asked.

'You are!' he said rather abruptly. 'But I shall return to my body and walk away from this place.'

'But how can you do that?' asked the young woman.

'I have the power,' Gordon said as he descended into his body. He said the strange word – but still nothing happened. He tried again. Again nothing happened.

When he floated out of his body again, the girl asked, 'Why have you not walked away from this place?'

'I don't know,' said Gordon, but when he looked down upon his naked body, he saw the reason why he was unable to return. The leather pouch full of ashes, black rose petals and dried leaves was missing.

'Oh, no!' he cried. 'They have taken my leather pouch.'

'Do not despair,' The young woman said, 'dead people do not need such things.'

'I am not dead!' Gordon shouted.

The young woman's spirit laughed gently and said, 'I did not believe it at first, but it is true. You must accept it.'

'I am not dead, I tell you!' Gordon argued.

But the girl was not listening. Instead she was looking ahead of her. Her ghostly face bathed in a soft, warm radiance. She said, 'I am coming now. I am ready.' And, slowly, her spirit faded away.

Gordon looked down upon his poor lifeless body and cried, 'I have been tricked and now Samuel has destroyed me too!' And then he wept a ghostly tear.

XIV

'Gordon,' his mother said, 'why are you so sad?'

He looked up at his mother and said, 'Because they have taken away my leather pouch and now I am unable to return to my body.'

'Even with the pouch it would be impossible, my son,' she said, 'for a priest has ministered the Last Rites over your body and no spirit may enter it.'

'Then I am dead, Mother?'

'Yes, my son. You are.'

'Mother! I tried to make something of myself, but I have failed you, and I have also done the most terrible things.'

'Yes, I know. And now I must show you exactly what you have done.' She waved her hand above her head and they were transported to someone's bedroom. Gordon did not recognise the room at first, but then the shopkeeper came in through the door and climbed into bed, whereupon his pillow immediately sprang to life and smothered his face. The shopkeeper struggled and struggled, but could not break free. Soon his spirit departed from his body with an agonising shriek, its face distorted beyond recognition, and then spirit and body both disappeared. After a few seconds, the whole scene repeated itself. This went on over and over again, and would continue to do so throughout eternity.

'This,' said Gordon's mother, 'is what that man's soul is condemned to. Are you happy with what you have done, Gordon?'

Gordon was not and said, 'No, Mother. I am not happy. This man should not have died and I feel much sorrow for what I have done to him.'

'Well, your sorrow is no comfort to the poor wretch now,' she said. 'Do you feel any sorrow for what you did to Samuel?'

'No! I feel no sorrow for that!' Gordon said. 'Not after the way he has destroyed me and my family.'

'Destroyed you, Gordon?' she said. 'What do you mean?'

'Just after you died, Mother, Samuel took my job away from me.'

'You are wrong, Gordon. Come, I will show you.' She waved her hand again and they were transported to Samuel's office.

XV

The door opened and in walked Samuel with the Managing Director. They were having an argument.

'I'm sorry, Sammy old boy,' said the Managing Director, 'I don't care if this Gordon What's-his-name is a friend of yours. He works in a section that we can no longer afford to operate, so he has got to go.'

Samuel said, 'But, sir! He is my best friend. Surely he could be transferred to another section?'

'No! It's quite out of the question,' the Managing Director replied. 'We cannot afford the cost of retraining him. Now there's an end to the matter.' The Managing Director then left the room and slammed the door behind him.

'Poor old Gordon,' said Samuel. 'How am I going to tell him?' Gordon's mother waved her hand and the scene disappeared.

'Well, why did he not tell me?' demanded Gordon.

'He was going to,' replied Gordon's mother, 'but when he bumped into you he was too upset to say anything.'

'But when I tried to get my job back he would not even see me.'

'That is what his secretary said, but Samuel did not know about it.'

'Well,' said Gordon, 'it was one of Samuel's companies that sent the bailiffs to throw me out of our home. How do you explain that?'

'He was on the board of directors, but he did not know about your eviction.'

'There is one thing I can never forgive him for,' said Gordon. 'Stealing Penelope away from me.'

'He did not steal her away from you at all. Penelope was not what she seemed Gordon. She really wanted to marry a man in a high position above all else, and when she met Samuel at a party she thought she had found the man that she had been looking for. Luckily, Samuel saw right through her charms and sent her packing with a flea in her ear.'

Gordon felt so confused. He did not know what to do. If his mother was right, he had killed the only true friend he had ever known. But then he remembered the dream that had started this whole crazy thing, in which he had discovered how Samuel had destroyed his whole family. He was about to tell his mother, but she anticipated what he was going to say and she waved her hand above her head.

XVI

Gordon was a young boy again. He was sitting down to dinner with his mother and father and brother Joe. They were eating a Christmas dinner and a huge log fire was blazing in the hearth.

'Gordon,' his father said, 'why are you so sad?'

'Because Samuel told you to go away. To stop loving us all,' Gordon replied.

'But this is untrue, my son. I have always loved you and I always will. The truth is that I did not run away. Times were hard and we had no money. I was forced to steal in order to feed us all. I was caught and sent to prison. Your mother did not want you to be ashamed of me, so she never told you.'

'Father, when will you return?'

'I will never return, Gordon. For when I was locked in my cell one night, there was a fire and I was burned to death. But remember – I will always love you all.' Having said this, his father disappeared, leaving behind a pile of dove feathers on the chair where he had been sitting.

'Gordon,' his bother Joe said, 'why are you so sad?'

'Because Samuel caused your death – and mine too, now,' Gordon replied.

'But this is untrue, my brother. Samuel was nowhere near when I died. He could not have possibly caused my death. The truth is that I never heeded the words of our wise mother. I was playing ball by the roadside when I dropped my ball and it rolled into the road. I never looked to see if anything was coming before I ran out into the road to fetch my ball. I was hit by a car and died instantly.' And, so saying, Joe disappeared, leaving behind a pile of sweet-smelling herbs on the chair where he had been sitting.

'Gordon,' his mother said (her voice was so weak that he had to put his ear close to her mouth to hear her words), 'why are you so sad?'

'Because Samuel prevented me from earning enough money to pay for your treatment. He hates me and wants to cause me nothing but misery,' Gordon replied.

'But that is untrue, my son. Samuel is the only true friend you have in this world. The truth is that there was no cure for me. I had no choice but to die.' With this said, his mother disappeared, leaving behind a pile of wishbones on the chair where she had been sitting.

Gordon gathered up the dove feathers and the sweet-smelling herbs and the wishbones and put them into a silk pouch that his mother had given him for Christmas. 'Oh Samuel! What have I done?' he sobbed. 'How can I undo this dreadful wrong I have done to you?'

'You can't!' bellowed the man. 'You have done my work well and now you are mine – forever!'

'Who are you?' Gordon demanded.

'You fool!' the man screamed. 'Haven't you guessed yet? Are you so stupid that you can't recognise Satan when you see him?'

Gordon trembled with fear as the man's head sprouted long, twisted horns and the eyes burned with a terrible fire – a fire fuelled by pure hatred. Gordon wanted to fight, but he had no weapon. He only had the silk pouch containing the dove feathers and the sweet-smelling herbs and the wishbones, and that would not stop a wild mouse, let alone the Devil himself.

Satan raised his arms above his hideous head and began summoning his minions. The flames in the fire grew bigger and took the form of strange beasts that leaped out onto the hearthrug, causing it to smoulder. The foundations of the whole house trembled with the awesome power Satan was using to call his slaves from the deepest, darkest corners of hell. The room filled with the stench of foul-smelling beasts and hideous forms of fearful proportions.

'Come!' Satan called. 'Come all you demons of hell! Come to welcome another into our midst! Let him discover suffering!' He laughed loud and long and the walls of the house started to crumble.

Gordon's fear and anger combined, and with all his might he let out a yell and hurled the silk pouch containing the dove feathers and the sweet-smelling herbs and the wishbones at Satan. It struck him right in the middle of his forehead. The silk pouch split open and the dove feathers fell onto the Devil's right shoulder. Satan shrieked with fear as Gordon's father appeared and said, 'Let these dove feathers represent the peace on Earth that will defeat your dark and evil forces.' Satan dropped to his knees.

Then the sweet-smelling herbs fell onto the Devil's left shoulder. Satan shrieked again and Gordon's brother Joe appeared and said, 'Let these sweet-smelling herbs represent the love that man has for his fellow man that will defeat your dark and evil forces.' Satan fell down onto his stomach.

Then the wishbones fell onto the floor beside the Devil's face. Gordon's mother appeared and said (in a loud and strong voice), 'Let these wishbones represent the hope of the future generations that will defeat your dark and evil forces.'

Satan cried out. He writhed on the floor in agony, but he was not finished yet. One more spirit was needed to defeat him, to turn him to water and send his minions fleeing back to his kingdom.

Samuel appeared standing over the Devil's prone body.

'Oh thank God!' cried Gordon. 'Help me! Help me, Samuel, my one true friend, to banish the Devil and save me from his eternal possession.'

Samuel's form was not a pretty sight. His flesh hung in ribbons from his bones, and his chest cavity was torn open to reveal only an empty space where his heart should have been. He appeared to ponder the situation for a few moments before he spoke, perhaps recalling the agonies of his death at the hands of his old school friend or a memory of their close friendship. 'Friend, I will help you,' he said. He then crouched down and continued speaking, 'Yes my friend, I will help you.' He dusted the dove feathers from the Devil's right shoulder; he dusted the sweet-smelling herbs from the Devil's left shoulder; he dusted the wishbones from the Devil's face; and gave his hand to help the Devil to his feet.

'Thank you, friend,' said the Devil and he smiled, pleased that revenge and hate had triumphed once again over friendship. And although he already had a collection of millions and millions of souls, he was always pleased to add two more, those of Samuel and Gordon, to it.

Back in the hospital mortuary, Gordon's body waited in a refrigerated metal drawer until, with post-mortem and registration of death completed, it would be buried in a multiple grave by the local council.

THE BOX

Sue Eaton

DAY 1

'What's this?' I ask as I study the curious box-like item, turning it over and over in my hands, as if that action would suddenly inspire the answer.

'What's what?' My wife doesn't take her eyes away from the computer screen.

'This,' I offer, holding out the box for her to see.

'What d'you mean this?'

'Just look at it, will you?'

'I'm working.'

'You're playing cards.'

'I'm having a break. I'm thinking.'

'How can you think about work while you're playing cards?'

'Because I can. I do lady-thinking. You should try it.'

I ignore her remarks, because otherwise the conversation will go round in circles – and she will win anyway. 'Look at this. Tell me what you think it is.'

'Yaay!' She bangs the keys in triumph. I can hear fireworks going off in the background. 'That was a bugger. What's that?'

I show her the box. 'I've no idea. I just found it outside on the front window sill. I thought you might have ordered something.'

She takes it from me, and turns it over and over as if it's

a Rubik's cube. It is roughly the same size as one. She pokes and presses it, but nothing happens. Finally she hands it back. 'It's pretty.'

'It's a plain metal box.'

'Well, it's shiny.' I refuse to get drawn in. 'A lot of people walk by our house on the way to the cut-through to the fields, so I suppose someone could have dropped it.'

'Then why was it on our window sill?'

'Perhaps someone thought it belonged to us.' The matter appears closed because my wife goes back at work, real work. I take the box and put it out on the front garden wall where people can see it. By the time I have made a pot of tea I have forgotten about it.

DAY 2

Shafts of clear, bright sunlight pierce the dimness of the room, and I throw back the curtains in the expectation of a glorious winter morning.

There it is. The box. On my window sill.

I stand stock still for long minutes, looking at it. What I expect it to do I cannot say, so eventually I give up and wander through to the kitchen to put the kettle on.

I can see my wife in the dining room as I pass the open door. Her face is lit by the glow of her laptop. She appears to be writing-working as opposed to thinking-working and I stay in the kitchen until the tea has brewed, then place her favourite mug quietly on the mat beside her.

'It's back.'

'Lovely, dear.'

'The box. It's back on the window sill.'

'That's nice.'

'Yes, dear,' I throw to the back of her head as I march

outside and slap the box firmly on the wall where everyone and his dog can see it.

'Morning, Bob.'

'Oh, morning, Bill.'

He acknowledges my attire. 'Taking it slower now you've retired?'

I pull my dressing gown over my pyjamas. 'Ha ha. Oh, yes. Er – you don't know who that might belong to, by any chance?' I indicate the box.

He takes a good look, weighing the box in first one hand and then the other. 'Never seen anything like that. I'd leave it on your wall if I was you. Someone will pick it up. You can't leave anything that isn't nailed down these days without it being nicked.'

'Good idea. Well, I'll let you get on. I've a cup of tea going cold indoors.'

'That won't be the only thing to go cold dressed like that. Get yourself inside, yer daft ha'p'orth.'

I watch him go, and then set about getting on with my day, but every so often I take a peek. The box is still there.

DAY 3

I peep gingerly around the curtain, and there it is, glowing in the early morning sun. I snap the material back in front of the window. If I can't see it, it isn't there.

'The damned box is back,' I snarl as I fill the kettle. There's no reply from the goodwife. She has her eyes fixed on the computer screen. 'I said, that damned...'

'I heard you. Stop stressing about the box. There're more important things to stress about if you really want something to do.' She taps a couple of keys before sitting back with a sigh. 'The possible outbreak of World War III, the starving millions and the fact that if I created a protagonist with a role and character like Donald Trump I'd be laughed out of every publishing house I contacted. But – hey ho – that's life and it's not fair.'

'At least that's a constant – life's never fair.'

'Right. As you've disturbed me, why don't you have a shower and get dressed, for a change? I'll pop to the shop and get some bacon and eggs and we'll start the day with a holiday breakfast.'

This is a ploy on my wife's behalf, for when I come back downstairs showered and dressed I see that the box has gone. It's not on the window sill and it's not on the wall. I stand and watch the cul-de-sac until I see her backing into the drive. 'Has someone picked up the box?' I ask as I open the door for her.

'No. It's in the bin. It's been here for days. Obviously no one wants it, so I've thrown it away.' She pushes through to the kitchen. 'Can you reach me the new bottle of oil? This one's empty.' Classic re-direction tactics.

I can't settle to anything, and find I'm constantly looking out of the window. There's no sign of the box, but I do get some funny looks from folk as they walk their dogs.

'Your problem is that you've nothing to do,' the goodwife comments as she brings me afternoon tea. 'You need to find a hobby.'

'I have a hobby.'

'Had. You had a hobby. You need to find something you can do now. Something staid you can do sitting down. Stressing about nothing won't do your heart any good.' She's right, of course, but it's easier said than done.

DAY 4

It's back! The bloody thing is back, sitting on my window sill as if it has every right to be there.

'What's up?' The goodwife spots the hammer I am wielding as I march through the house and bang open the front door. I throw the box to the ground in full view of neighbours and dog walkers alike, and swing the hammer with as much might as I can. It bounces off the smooth surface sending waves of pain up through my arm and across my chest.

'For God's sake, stop it! Stop it this minute.' My wife looks as ashen as I feel. 'You'll have another heart attack if you carry on like this.' She takes the hammer from me and picks up the box, at the same time elbowing me in the back. 'Tea, now!'

She keeps giving me surreptitious looks over her tea mug as we sit with the box between us.

'What?'

'Nothing. I'm just thinking.'

'You're thinking that I might have fished the bastard thing out of the bin, aren't you? What the bloody hell do you think I am?'

'Well, you've not been well, dear.'

'I've had a frigging heart attack not a mental breakdown. I can do without this.'

'Of course, dear,' she soothes. 'I'm going to take it and dispose of it when I've drunk my tea. I shan't tell you where. I want you to forget all about it.' She stares at the box for long seconds. 'We'll go somewhere nice for lunch when I get back. My treat.'

She's gone for quite a while – not to the local tip, then. I look anxiously at her on her return, but her face gives nothing away. 'There, that's seen the back of that,' she says as she hangs her coat on its customary peg. 'No more box.'

She chooses The Lamb, a favourite pub of mine, but despite the friendly discourse and heavenly food I cannot settle. I prod at my vegetables with my fork, deep in thought. Am I going quietly mad or is it the world around me?

Sod the bloody box.

DAY 5

'What on earth are you doing sitting in the dark?' I haven't the energy to answer. 'Bob?' I turn my gaze to the tightly drawn curtains. My wife shakes her head and with a flourish draws them back to let in the grey murk of this particular morning.

'What the …?' She turns and looks at me.

'I don't know where you took it. It wasn't me that bought it back.'

The box is glowing in the half light, as if reflecting some unseen source of power. She goes into the hall and checks the silver dish on the hall stand. The car keys are there. Not that that signifies anything, really, other than I may have deviated from a lifetime of putting them in my pocket rather than leaving them in the dish for her to use.

'You don't believe me. I'm not allowed to drive yet, you know. Not for another couple of weeks.'

'I had to check. There's got to be some logical explanation for this.' She stares at me. 'Someone must have more than one box. You haven't pissed anyone off lately, have you?'

'What d'you mean?'

'Well, I know you. You expect everything done the way

you would do it and complain if it isn't. This could be someone getting their own back.'

'I've not been out on my own, apart from the garden. Not since the heart attack.'

She thinks for a minute, knowing I'm right. 'I'm going to hang on to the bloody thing myself,' she says. 'If I've got it, no one can have it. I'll put a stop to this nonsense.'

She disappears for quite a while. I remain sitting in the armchair; I haven't the energy to move. Whoever is doing this is making me ill and I don't need it.

'Don't ask,' she says on her return.

'I wasn't going to. I want this over.'

'Annette and John are coming over this afternoon to see you. That'll take your mind of things.'

Annette and John get right up my bum crack, but just this once it might be for the best. Seeing if I can be sarcastic without them noticing will engage my mind in a far better way than mithering about the box, however shiny it is.

DAY 6

In the small hours I can't sleep, so get up for a cup of tea. I mooch about and play a couple of games on the goodwife's computer, read what she's written, decide my brain isn't big enough for it, and go back to bed to attempt to sleep. I finally drop off after she gets up. My wife rises at unheardoff o'clock in order to write before the world wakes and breaks her train of thought, and I tend to stay out of the way.

This morning I don't wake until the sun is well and truly up, and as it's January that is quite late. I stagger downstairs in search of tea, barely noticing that the front room door is firmly shut. My wife is sitting at her computer in a pose that suggests thinking-working, but something about her posture bothers me.

'Are you alright?'

'Come here.' She has her large battered cashbox in which she keeps receipts for the accountant and the moneybox she had as a very young child lined up in front of her. She looks scared and points to the cashbox. 'I locked the box in there, and because you know I keep the key in my knicker drawer I dropped it in the moneybox.'

'But you don't know the combination to the moneybox.'

'I know, and neither do you.' She shakes the box and I hear something rattling. 'The key is still there.' She picks up the cashbox in both hands and gives it a shake. There is no sound; it's obviously empty. 'Go look on the window sill.' I can't. I sit heavily on the nearest chair.

'I thought that you might have been doing it at first, because I'm spending so much time on my book. Then I thought someone might be doing it as a joke. That they might have a few boxes. I mean, I threw that one yesterday in a skip in the city dump. Not even the local one.' I nod because I don't know what else to do. 'This is spooky.' I nod again. Because she likes spooky, my wife has a plan. 'We'll leave it on the window sill and ignore it. In fact, we could look on one of those late room sites and go away for a few days, see what occurs. You haven't an appointment until the end of next week, so it's feasible.' It's shaken her though.

I'm all for this, which is why we are now on our way to York for a midweek break in the middle of winter with snow threatening.

DAYS 7-8

We are away.

DAY 9

York was mostly shut, but we found a nice little hotel and spent a lot of the time, snug and warm, reading in one pub or another. No one bothered us and I began to feel a little more like my old self – before the heart attack. I even managed to put the box into some sort of perspective. It was a joke on someone's part. If I ignored it, they would soon get tired and either give up or arrive on the doorstep with a daft explanation and a 'Wasn't it a hoot?' To which I will reply, 'No,' and shut the door in their face.

It is quite late and dark on arriving home. The goodwife is desperate for a wee and I am very tired, so we hurry indoors, out of the drizzle. I shall sort the cases in the morning; now, I am ready for bed.

DAY 10

The front room door is shut as I come downstairs. 'Stay away from the door,' says a disembodied voice from the dining room.

I peer into the gloom. The goodwife is sitting at the computer, but she is not working; even I can see that. 'It's still there?' I ask. She nods. 'Well, like you said, we'll leave it and see what occurs,' I suggest and go and make a cup of tea.

Once dressed, I go to the car to fetch the cases and bags, totally ignoring the window sill. I have to make two journeys because the shops in the Shambles weren't shut and my wife made a number of purchases: things she couldn't possibly live without. I am determined not to look, but it is a lovely day, the drizzle gone and the sun brilliant as only winter sun can be. A shaft of light hits me in the eye as I turn from the car on the second of my journeys. It takes my attention straight to the box.

I have an urge to pick it up and stroke the smooth, cool sides. I shake my head. 'Bloody fool,' I tell myself. I slam indoors, and take the cases upstairs, but once in the bedroom I find myself at the window, contorting to see if I can make out the box on the window sill directly below me. It's an impossible task and attempting it, I knock into the dressing table and overturn a perfume bottle, which cracks onto the surface, rolls round and round until it drops onto the wooden floor and with a resounding crash shatters into a million pieces.

'What the bloody hell?' demands the wife as she hurries into the bedroom. What can I tell her that she doesn't know already? That I'm a bigger arse than even she thought?

DAY 11

It's a cold, drizzly sort of morning and the box is still there. I take my tea into the front room and sit on the back of the settee and stare out at the box. I have this overwhelming feeling of sadness, and shiver slightly. It is certainly not cold in our house and I am snuggly dressed in warm pyjamas and fleecy dressing gown. I am not cold; the box is cold – and sad. The longer I sit, the more convinced I am that I need to bring it inside into the warmth. I don't even feel daft. I just have a need to comfort the box.

I quietly open the front door and snatch the shiny thing from the window sill. I walk soundlessly into the kitchen and rub it dry with the hand towel, warm from the radiator. Just for a moment I expect a genie to appear and chuckle as I look around for somewhere to keep the pretty, shiny object. The goodwife is busy writing and pays no heed to what I am doing as long as I don't disturb her, so I mooch about the house looking for somewhere to display it.

It doesn't like the kitchen very much and I daren't go into the dining room until allowed, so we look in the front room. It's all a bit pristine in there as we rarely use it, so I try upstairs. It quite likes the 'Home Office' as my wife calls her writing room. She stopped using it after I was taken ill, as she likes to keep her eye on me. I place it on the window sill overlooking the back garden and sit in the computer chair and watch it for a while.

I wake to the sound of my wife calling me as if from some distance. I am in a very strange but immensely beautiful place and really don't want to leave. I fight against the voice, pushing it to the back of my consciousness, trying to concentrate on the exquisite world I find myself in, but to no avail. My wife's sharp, insistent tone breaks through, and suddenly I am back in the computer chair, shivering.

'Are you alright? I was worried about you. You're not feeling ill, are you?'

'For God's sake, woman,' I snap, forcing her to step back. 'Can't you leave me a-fucking-lone for one minute?'

'I'm sorry. I'm sure. There's no need to be so rude.' She doesn't like me swearing.

There's no way I can go back to sleep now, but I convince myself I will not apologise. I was happy in my dream world, and now I feel empty, as if I have been snatched from something wonderful. She can go rot for all I care.

DAY 12

'Have you been there all night?' The sharp tones shatter my concentration.

'No, I've been to the loo twice.'

'Don't be facetious; you know what I mean.'

I can't hear what the box is saying to me; it shut down when she walked in.

'Shove the fuck off, will you? I can't concentrate.' There's silence for a moment.

'Are you alright, Bob?' I don't answer in case I encourage her to stay. 'Do you need anything?' I remain fixed on the box. I feel the draught as she leaves and the quiet click as the door shuts behind her. I expect she will interrupt me with a mug of tea shortly. I concentrate. Now that the box has started to communicate with me, I am anxious to hear its message.

I have been having vivid dreams since I brought the box inside. I am in a wonderful city where everything is clean and peaceful, but it seems as if I am there in spirit only. I see people, but I can't communicate with them, and they don't seem to realise that I am there. The architecture is like nothing I have seen before, not on this Earth or in any films I have watched. I am comfortable there and don't want to leave. With every corner I turn, I am expecting something: I don't know what, but it will be fabulous.

'Bob?' The bloody wife keeps dragging me back.

'What did I tell you?' I snarl at the door.

'I've brought you tea.'

'I don't want any fucking tea.'

'There's no need to swear, dear. I'll leave it here – by the door.'

It's still early, but I know it won't be long before she's on the phone and then the peace will be gone. The box tells me not to worry, that it's not going anywhere and then it shuts down. I am absurdly angry, like the time I gave up smoking and had to fight the cravings. I suddenly realise I am having withdrawal symptoms. I am yearning for interaction with the box. I want to know what it wants, what it expects of me. I am ready to comply, but my wife is stopping me. We'll have to see what we can do about that, won't we?

DAY 13

I expected my wife to ring the medics yesterday, but no one disturbed me, so I can only assume she rang her sister instead. Sister-in-law would have told her to let the silly sod stew in his own juice. Good for her.

I drift in and out of my dreamworld, exploring a little further each time. I am fascinated by the soaring architecture and the vividness of the colours. The people I see seem happy and stress-free. They wander through the streets with smiles for their fellow man, instead of rushing about with mobile phones glued to their ears.

I see what looks like a park and am about to enter when my wife's discordant voice breaks through and I find myself back in the Home Office feeling bereft. I stare at her. I feel so deprived I am unable to speak. I am holding the box and for some reason I feel compelled to pass it to my wife.

'What?' she asks, but she takes it anyway. 'What am I supposed to do with this?'

'Listen to it,' I tell her in all seriousness.

'Is it making noises now?' She holds the box away from her.

'Just listen. Tell me if you hear anything.'

She puts the box to her right ear; she's a little deaf in the left. She listens for a while and then gives it a little shake. 'What am I supposed to hear?'

'I don't know.'

'You don't know? What's the matter with you?' But she puts the box back to her ear.

What happens next defies telling. I sit and look at the box. It is still the size of a Rubik's cube and doesn't appear to have any form of opening, but a tiny black hole slowly whirls open and sucks my wife inside as if she is nothing but air. I watch her go. I see the expression of complete shock on her face as she does so; first her ear and then her head stretches and her eyes widen. I see the perfect O of her mouth before it disappears; then with a smooth slurp, the rest of her body. There is nothing left, no trace.

The box is much happier now; bigger, I think. I can feel it sated and content. It sits on the Home Office window sill and looks over the back garden. I watch it and wonder how long it will be before it becomes hungry again.

IT'LL ROT YOUR TEETH

Wondra Vanian

'I can't believe we're doing this!' Ella giggled as they walked away from a house where they had been given handfuls of sweets.

Clutching her hand tightly, Millie ducked behind Ella as they passed a tall boy in a bloody hockey mask.

'It's scary,' she said.

Bumping Millie's shoulder playfully, Ella said, 'It's *supposed* to be scary, silly. It's Halloween.'

But their mother was Llanolaeth's only dentist and, some would say, a little obsessed with good oral hygiene. The closest either girl had ever got before to the sickening sweetness of Halloween was watching their mother cooking up bowl after bowlful of sugar-free boiled sweets to disappoint children foolish enough to think that Mrs Jenkins's house was a good place to trick-or-treat.

Sneaking out had been Ella's idea. She was tired of her classmates bragging about their 'Halloween hauls'. Tired of watching them pass fun-sized chocolate bars to one another during lunch while she chewed on carrot sticks. Of stupid Rhian Morgan sucking loudly on her Double Lolly as she asked Ella what *she'd* done the night before.

It was common knowledge that the Jenkins girls weren't allowed to trick-or-treat. Or accept cake when someone in the class celebrated a birthday. Or eat ice cream in the summer, candy canes at Christmas, or chocolate eggs at Easter. Adults gave the girls sympathetic looks while commenting on their beautiful, strong teeth.

Kids just laughed and called them freaks.

Millie was only four. She was too young to understand what she was missing out on. But Ella was seven and three quarters – old enough to realise how different they were from other kids. So, when Ella saw the costume hanging in the back of her closet, made for last year's Nativity Play, she came to a decision.

There weren't many angels on the streets of Llanolaeth that night – at least, not little angels like Ella. She did see some older girls, though, in costumes she doubted very much angels would wear. There weren't any other lambs at all.

Ella had expected her sister to complain that the costume was too tight – she'd grown a whole two inches since Christmas – or that it was a stupid costume for Halloween, but Millie did neither. She just shrugged her shoulders, said okay, and pulled on the woolly jumper. Digging a couple of old pillowcases out of the closet in the hallway, Ella had taken Millie's hand and, together, they'd crept quietly through the house, into the garage, and out into the night.

Halloween was magical. For the first time in her life, Ella joined the throngs of children who laughed as they ran from house to house, bags extended to accept the handfuls of brightly-wrapped sweets tossed their way. She tore into toffee, chomped on Flying Saucers, and tossed back tiny sachets of sherbet.

She got to experience, first hand, what her classmates had meant when they said, 'sugar high.' Grinning broadly,

Ella bounced along, dragging her more reluctant sister behind.

'Mummy will be mad if she finds out we're not in bed,' the younger girl said as they made their way to the next house. There was a whine to her voice that normally meant a trembling lip would soon follow.

Ella glanced down. Millie shuffled behind, dutifully but not happily. One woolen-mittened hand tugged at a floppy black ear.

'What's wrong, lamb?'

Millie's eyes, when she looked up, were misty. 'I don't want Mummy to be mad at us,' she said.

Ella's excitement waned a little. The smile Millie had worn when they received their first handful of sweets was gone, replaced by a look of childish worry.

'Okay, lamb,' Ella told her, 'let's head home.'

Millie's mood only lifted when they were back in their pyjamas, sitting on the floor of the bedroom they shared, with a pile of sweeties spread out on a pillowcase between them. 'I like this one best,' she told Ella, offering her the other half of a Bounty Miniature, a chocolate bar filled with coconut.

Ruin perfectly good candy with fruit? Ella screwed up her face. She handed Millie one with honeycomb instead.

'*Ych a fi.* Try this one. It's—'

The bedroom door swinging open preceded their mother's entrance by no more than a few seconds. Ella used that time to throw her empty pillowcase over the pile. Following her lead, Millie scooted in front of it.

'What are you girls doing up?' their mother asked with a frown.

Neither girl was a natural liar; they were both too afraid of their mother to try, normally. But sneaking out, trick-or-treating, and eating sweets or chocolate were all big, big no-nos. If they *didn't* lie, they were sure to get a good whack with the cane that hung in the kitchen.

So they lied.

'Millie had a bad dream,' Ella said in a hurry. 'She couldn't get back to sleep so I was trying to cheer her up.' She looked to her sister for confirmation.

'Uh huh. A bad dream.'

Their mother wore a suspicious look but nodded. 'Well,' she said, 'you girls hurry up and get back in bed.' Both girls breathed a sigh of relief as she turned to leave.

It was too soon.

Something under Ella's bed caught their mother's eye. Bending down, she picked the thing up and held it up for them to see. It was an empty Maltesers Teasers wrapper. Millie gasped, covering her mouth with a hand.

Ella was on her feet before her mother could say anything. 'Please don't be mad at Millie,' she pleaded. 'I made her do it. She didn't want to.' Millie sniffled behind her.

At first, their mother said nothing. Waiting was *awful*. Ella's stomach tied itself in so many knots it felt like all the sweets she'd eaten were trying to force their way back out.

Stepping around Ella, their mother tugged the pillowcase off the mound of forbidden sweets. Her eyes burned hot and angry. A muscle jerked in her cheek as she ground her teeth together.

'Where did you get this?'

Lying wasn't going to get them out of this. 'I snuck out,' Ella told her mother. 'I went trick-or-treating and I brought back sweets for us share.'

Millie was shaking her head, tears running down her nose. She wouldn't let her sister take all the blame. 'No,

Mummy,' she said. 'I—'

'Shut up.'

Millie bit her lip. Ella's knees trembled so hard they practically knocked together.

Their mother pinched the bridge of her nose between her fingers. 'I am so disappointed in you,' she said. 'Both of you.'

'How many times do I have to tell you? This stuff is poison. It'll rot your teeth. But you don't care, do you?' She didn't give them time to argue. 'You'd rather eat this filthy rubbish than have teeth when you're adults, is that it?'

Both Millie and Ella said no, of course not, but their mother wasn't listening.

'Well, that's your choice,' she said. 'But you have to know the consequences. Downstairs, both of you. Now.'

Reluctantly, they followed their mother out of the room and down the stairs. Ella took Millie's hand a gave it a reassuring squeeze. It wasn't the first time either of them had got the cane from their mother — but that didn't make it any easier.

But, when they entered the kitchen, their mother didn't reach for the wooden cane that hung by the door. Instead, she motioned for them to sit at the counter. Silicone moulds were spread across the surface, some full of cooling sweets, some waiting for the mixture that bubbled on the stove.

Shaking her head, their mother said, 'I've done everything in my power to protect you. To keep you safe and healthy while those dirty little pigs out there stuff themselves full of poison. And you...'

She turned away and Millie groped blindly for Ella's hand. Ella took it and held tightly. When their mother returned, she held one of the large plastic bowls filled with her homemade sugar-free boiled sweets. The girls exchanged a look; it wasn't the punishment they had been expecting.

'I know I told you that this was for the trick-or-treaters only,' their mother told them, 'but you should have some.'

Neither Ella nor Millie moved.

'I'm not hungry,' Millie said in a tiny voice.

Laughing bitterly, their mother said, 'Stuffed yourself full of chocolate, did you? Well, that's just too bad, because you're going to have some. Both of you.'

With a nervous glance at her sister, Ella reached for one of the cellophane-wrapped sweets. Her fingers shook so hard that she nearly couldn't open it. Her mother stared hard at her until Ella popped the sweet into her mouth. Millie followed suit.

The sweet was hard, like the butter mints Ella had just learned she loved, but not as sweet. It tasted of apple, with a hint of some other flavour that Ella couldn't name. Not as bad as she'd expected – but not as nice as the sweets upstairs.

Ella's mouth started to burn.

'May I have a glass of water, please?' she asked.

Millie nodded. 'Me too, please.'

Their mother only stared at them, crossing her arms across her chest. 'Another,' she said.

Ella didn't want another. She felt... funny. Sick, but not like the cold she'd had back in the spring. Or like that time she had the chicken pox. She felt *wrong* sick. Her teeth and throat hurt and her stomach squeezed hard. She felt hot but cold too. A look at her sister's sweaty face told Ella that she wasn't the only one feeling unwell.

The doorbell chimed.

With a sigh, their mother shoved the bowl toward the girls. 'Another,' she repeated.

Ella struggled to open the second sweet; her fingers fumbled with the cellophane. Finally, she got it open. She couldn't seem to close her mouth around it, though. Her jaw wasn't moving correctly and her tongue tasted bad.

Millie sobbed loudly.

The doorbell chimed again. Their mother picked up the bowl and went to greet the trick-or-treaters. Millie's hand went slack in Ella's and, when she turned, Ella found her sister on the floor. Millie's mouth and chin were covered in blood and something in a shade of yellow that just *couldn't* be good.

No, Ella realised. Not Millie's mouth and chin.

Millie didn't have either. They'd rotted away to nothing but bone and burning flesh. A noise somewhere between a wheeze and a whimper issued from her throat – which was also sizzling away.

Everything went fuzzy as Ella slid to the floor beside her sister. She reached for Millie but didn't quite make it. Her arm flopped uselessly on the floor, strength seeping from her body in a pool of blood and pus. The last thing Ella saw was the rotten cavity that was once her sister's beautiful smile.

* * *

The events of that Halloween night in Llanoleath dominated all the frontpages of the national press and every news bulletin for months. Nobody had ever known anything like it. It was as if the whole country were in mourning and shock. And it seemed as if Llanoleath had only just stopped being the centre of the national media's attention when, just before the next Halloween, the town was once again descended upon by camera crews.

'Olivia Roberts reporting here, from the steps of Llanolaeth Civic Centre, where a curfew order has just been approved, banning children from going out on the night of October 31st, effectively ending Halloween celebrations within the county.'

The camera followed Roberts as she passed a group – mostly youths, naturally – of protesters. She stopped beside a plump woman holding a sign that read, 'Halloween doesn't kill, people kill!'

'I'm here with Theresa Roberts, who believes the new law fails to address the real problem. Is that correct, Theresa?'

'That's right,' Theresa said loudly, staring down the camera like it was the barrel of a gun. 'It's like putting a plaster on a severed limb and expecting everything to be okay.'

The reporter nodded, wearing an expression that said she was listening intently to the other woman.

'The media's got so wrapped up in all this Halloween rubbish that they forgot there's still a killer on the loose. If someone is sick enough to poison twenty-seven innocent children, why should we believe a curfew will do any good?'

Her voice rose as her speech became more impassioned. 'Somewhere, out there,' Theresa said, 'wandering the streets of Llanolaeth, there's a sick person who needs to be held accountable for their actions. Find that person. Make them pay. *That* is what we should be doing, not blaming a harmless bit of fun like trick-or-treating.'

'Thank you, Theresa,' the reporter said. 'Thank you.'

Olivia turned to speak directly to the camera. 'It's been a long, painful campaign for the members of Parents Against Halloween.'

She walked away from the protesters, stopping beside a tall, slim woman in a trousersuit. 'Here with me now is Mrs Jenkins, whom many of our local viewers will recognise as Llanolaeth's own dentist.

'This is a very important day for you, Mrs Jenkins. I understand you lost both of your children the night of the Halloween Massacre.'

Mrs Jenkins nodded sadly.

'Yes,' she told the reporter. 'There are no words to describe how it feels to lose a child.'

Swallowing hard, Mrs Jenkins continued, 'It's the most devastating thing possible, to wake up in a world that doesn't include your beautiful daughters anymore.' A tear ran down her cheek. 'It's even worse when you know that you're the reason they're no longer with you.'

'Do I understand you correctly, Mrs Jenkins?' the reporter asked. 'Do you somehow blame yourself for The Massacre?'

Mrs Jenkins nodded. 'Completely,' she said. 'Didn't I hand them the sweets? Didn't I tell them to eat them?'

She turned her attention to the camera for the first time. 'Didn't we all? Aren't we all to blame?

'As a nation, we've allowed this dangerous institution to invade our homes, our towns, our country. Why? Why emulate a country that's as deeply flawed as America? Let them keep their so-called traditions,' she said, 'I would much rather keep our children safe. That's why I started Parents Against Halloween. It's been a long, hard year for us. We've had to battle people who would rather let their children die than let go of America's coattails.'

Mrs Jenkins's eyes blazed with passion. 'Maybe there is a psychopath roaming the streets of Llanolaeth,' she said. 'Maybe it was nothing more sinister than a terrible accident in a factory somewhere – the investigation is still underway. We may never know what caused The Massacre. What we do know is this: You can't hand your child poison and not expect it to kill them. If we force Halloween to release its hold on our children, we are taking that poison away from them. If I had to lose both my daughters, to save every other child in Llanolaeth— Well,' Mrs Jenkins concluded, 'I have to say it's worth it.'

The camera swung back to the reporter.

'There you have it,' Olivia said. 'Llanolaeth's new Halloween curfew might be dividing opinion but – according to one mother – it's saving our children. Back to the studio.'

THE ROSE

Suzan St Maur

The gravel hitting the window caused me to wake with a start. I felt my way over to it, curled back the curtain and looked out. Goodness me. Silly lad. I silently raised the sash.

'I thought you were going back to the base tonight!'

'I was. I did,' Will stage-whispered. 'Then I went out again. Back door, so to speak.'

'Ooh, naughty.'

'It gets naughtier. Our lot's been postponed till tomorrow night. Come on down, it's ever so nice out.'

I quickly threw on my shirt and Land Army trousers. Not the most romantic look to go and meet your beau on an English summer's night, but there was no time to dress up. I crept down the stairs and out the front door.

'Allo, my gorgeous Meg.' Before I could draw breath he had kissed me hard for several beautiful seconds. 'Come on, let's go up the park.'

He lit two cigarettes and passed one to me as we settled down on the damp grass. 'There's talk of an invasion, pet. Going to get in there and give Jerry a damned good hiding.'

I could feel my body tensing up. 'When's that going to be then?'

For a few seconds we gazed at the red tips of our cigarettes glowing in the gloom. 'Can't say, pet. Top secret.

But us lot's going over there first to soften them up, like.'

Must be a really heavy bombing campaign, I thought. Please God let him come home safe. Please.

'Cat got your tongue? Are you alright?'

I nestled my face in the roughness of his uniform.

'Come on, pet. War'll be over soon.'

I started to cry softly.

'We'll have old Jerry whipped in no time. You'll see. Then when I'm home p'raps we shall get engaged.'

'I love you, Will Prentice.'

'Show me how much.'

He slid a hand under my shirt, then skilfully dealt with the buttons on my trousers. 'I hope there's no nettles round here,' I giggled.

'You won't notice them if there is any,' Will said in a hoarse voice as he manoeuvred us round. We joined together, our passion heightened by the threat of being discovered in the park – and of impending danger beyond. For what seemed like a lifetime we crested our wave, two people as one, light years away from the awfulness of war.

Afterwards we lay quietly, listening to the rustles and croaks of an early summer night. Our breathing was synchronised, our hearts beat in time. A warm breeze tickled our skin. Neither of us wanted even to whisper for fear of bursting the bubble.

'Fancy a smoke, pet?' Will reached for his trousers, and after some fumbling produced two lit Senior Services. We smoked silently, cuddling together and watching the stars.

'What's it like up there, Will?'

'What, in the Lancs? Bit weird, like. I'm always going backwards.'

'Silly, that's because you're a rear gunner. Is it really scary though?'

'Tell you what, it's ruddy cold up there.'

'How cold?'

'Oh, minus forty or so. That's at thirty-odd thousand feet.'

'Horrible. And even more scary.'

'Isn't much time to get scared when you've got Jerry's paper darts coming up at you out of nowhere. That's when I pick 'em off. Ratta-tatta-tatta-tatta-tatta...'

'Shhhh, Will, someone will hear us.'

Will sniggered.

'Aren't you frightened then? When you're up there?'

'Don't be a silly goose. Those Lancs are stronger than tanks. It'd take more than a few poncey little Messerschmitts to do us any damage. And we fly way above the ACAC. Don't even come close.'

'I hope you're right, Will.'

'Better go back now, pet. Be getting light soon and I don't want no Squadron Leader spotting me shinning up that drainpipe.'

'Drainpipe?'

''Course. Right by the window. Easy as pie. Might a bit harder going back up than coming down, mind.'

'You be careful,' I said as we adjusted our clothes, and set off back towards the High Street.

'I'll see you in six weeks,' Will said after we had kissed and embraced for a long time. 'You behave yourself now, young lady.'

'Stay safe, Will. I love you.'

'And I love you, pet. Oh, wait up. Got something for you.'

Will reached into his jacket and pulled out a single red rose. 'Here.'

'Oh, Will, it's beautiful.'

'Pinched it out of the park, but don't tell anyone. Must go now, pet. Tara.'

Holding the rose carefully against my face, I watched him walk away in the growing dawn. As his image faded into the distance, I heard the familiar growls and groans of the Lancs coming back to base. Then they were there, overhead. I could make out bits of damage on some, coughing, spluttering misfiring engines, smoke streaming out behind them. Stay safe Will. Please.

Creeping carefully into the house, I placed the red rose gently on my pillow. I crawled under the coverlet, cried a little, inhaled the fresh scent of the rose, then fell asleep.

I woke up rather late and stumbled downstairs to fetch the post. I felt dreadfully hungover. Strange. I hadn't had any alcohol the previous day. I opened the front door to get some air.

'Morning, Miss,' said an elderly female voice. 'You must be the new girl what's in the Varley's old house.'

'Yes, hello,' I said, wishing this conversation could take place when my head wasn't throbbing like a diesel engine and my brain was functioning a bit more clearly than a raging blizzard.

'What did you say your name was, love?'

I hadn't, but OK. Just answer briefly and perhaps she'll go away. 'I'm Meg.'

'How funny. Oh, manners. I'm Elizabeth Prentice. That's Miss, as it were. Never married. Anyway, my brother was in love with the Varley's daughter here. Her name was Meg.'

'Really? Where is he now?'

'Dead, my dear. Killed. Only 25. In the RAF, he was.

Lancaster bomber in 1944. Just before D Day. Shot down in flames, so they said.' She sniffed.

'I'm so sorry. Would you excuse me, Miss Prentice? I really must have a look at something.' Something jangled in among the cacophony of white noise in my head.

Without knowing why, I walked over to the flower bed immediately under my bedroom window, where just that weekend Mum had dug out the weeds and raked it over ready for her geraniums.

Gravel. A good handful or two splattered about in the neat soil. It could have been worse. There were idiots who would chuck McDonald's cartons and used condoms and God knows what else just anywhere. Like on people's flower beds. So much for being PC and all the careful recycling of the 21st century, eh? But even though it was only gravel this time, Mum would still have a fit.

My head hurt. Not so much throbbing as knocking, nudging. A memory trying to get through. What? Oh come on, brain. Clear up.

I went inside. Just have a shower and never mind the gravel. I hauled myself up the stairs and sat down on my bed. Now the room started to spin and I felt sick. Must lie down. Lie down. Head on the pillow. Eyes shut. Keep still.

Something lightly scratched my cheek. Ouch.

I turned my head and inhaled deeply. I could smell something beautifully perfumed. Instantly my head cleared and the pain disappeared.

It all came back to me.

I opened my eyes and began to shiver.

Next to me on the pillow was a single, fresh red rose.

DOING TIME

Martin S. Beckley

'I can't do this anymore.' The words dribbled from my mouth in a repressed whisper.

'Do what dear?'

Her feigned ignorance added to the growing tightness in my stomach. How could such a frail old lady command so much fear in me? I fixed my gaze on the foot of her bed – if I looked at her, I would lose. I sensed her watching me – she knew, she knew what I wanted to say. The sudden flush to my face startled me. My throat constricted as if she had the power to prevent me from speaking.

'What's the matter?' she taunted. 'Cat got your tongue?'

I did not need to look; I could feel victory radiating from her. It felt hot, it felt sharp, and it pierced every part of my body.

'Here, go refill this, there's a good girl.' She waved the hot-water bottle at me. The faded Winnie-the-Pooh cover smiled reassuringly at me. I took the bottle and retreated downstairs.

In the semi-darkness, I filled the kettle and switched it on. I pulled back the yellowing net curtain and peered at the lifeless grey sky. Hugging the cold hot-water bottle, I unlocked the back door and stepped into the small footnote of a garden. No grass grew in this concrete-slab enclosure;

the only colour came from the mass of ivy that smothered the crumbling brickwork marking out the boundary. A soft rain caressed my face as I gazed longingly at the horizon. Brooding thunderclouds made their remorseless advance.

'Come on,' I said to the Pooh water bottle, 'let's fill you up.'

Dad had given him to me for my fifth birthday. Two months later I lost a massive part of my life – my dad died. One morning my dad kissed me on the head and said, 'See you later honey pot, love you lots,' as he always did and left the house. I didn't see him again. Mother would not allow me to go to his funeral. I didn't get a chance to say goodbye. I hated her for that.

I returned to my dungeon, leaving the fresh air and gentle rain behind me. 'Oh Pooh, if only we could escape.'

'Go now!' said Pooh. His soft, deep voice always reminded me of calming lullabies, warm summer evenings and the smell of mints. Dad loved eating mints. Pooh always uses Dad's voice when he talks to me. Renewed with hot water, I hugged him close. His fresh warmth stinging my arms and chest through my thinning dress, I did not care.

'You know she won't let me go,' I told him.

'Just go. Walk out the door now.'

'I can't, not without telling her I'm going. What would she say?'

'It doesn't matter, just go.'

'I can't; she needs me.'

'She uses you.'

The clanging of Mother's hand bell interrupted us. I ran to the foot of the stairs.

'Agony! Agony! Make me a pot of tea, there's a good little girl.'

I bit into my lower lip so hard this time I could feel my teeth puncture the flesh.

'Did you hear me, Agony?'

'Yes, sorry Mother,' I called, and then under my breath, 'My name is Agnes!' I stomped back to my dungeon. An itching heat stabbed at my neck dominating my thoughts. I tried scratching but my bitten nails were useless. I rolled up my sleeve and bit into my arm until the pain distracted me from the heat on my neck. I stared at the reddening depressions in my pallid skin. 'I hate you,' I whispered, 'I hate you, I hate you, I hate you.' I flicked the kettle back on and then, flushing slightly, hid the bite mark from Pooh. He did not say anything but I knew he did not approve. 'I'm sorry Pooh, please talk to me.'

Nothing.

'I couldn't help it ... I'm sorry.'

Nothing.

'Please talk to me ... tell me what to do.'

Nothing.

I rubbed my arm. He was ashamed of me. He knew I could not stand the silence. 'Don't shut me out ... I'll stand up to her ... I promise ... I'll tell her I'm leaving.' The kettle came to the boil. 'I'll take her tea up first.' Thunder grumbled in the distance.

The gloomy staircase was just wide enough to carry the tray without scraping my knuckles. The steep incline was barely manageable; the shallow treads forcing me to balance on half a foot. 'I'm going to tell her,' I whispered to Pooh tucked under my arm. My feet felt heavy; each step took more effort than the last. 'But I'll need your support, Pooh.'

The tray seemed to gain a pound in weight with each step I climbed. Four steps from the top and the frightening scent of lavender talcum powder flooded my nostrils. Oh my God, she's out of bed. Where is she? What has she done? The tray shook in my hands. The once bearable heat from the water bottle now felt like thousands of pins piercing my skin. The staircase suddenly darkened. Fat, heavy rain attacked the window at the top of the stairs. Mother's hand bell rang out like the bell on a buoy warning sailors not to get too close.

'Agony!' Clang. 'Where are you, girl?' Clang, clang. 'Agony!' Clang, clang, clang.

What had she done to herself this time? Past traumas surfaced in terrifying succession:

I was home from school, ready for my sixteenth birthday sleepover, and found Mother unconscious in a bath of ice water. My eighteenth birthday, I had booked a weekend away with some friends. Mother sliced her hand with the bread knife. She saw off any boys who paid me any attention. Except for Michael. He stuck around and when I was twenty-three, he proposed. Mother held a hot iron to her arm until I promised to reject him.

'Agony, what are you doing out there?' Light exploded into the insignificant no-man's land of the landing. The stairs trembled beneath my feet as the overpowering blast of thunder assaulted the tiny house. Once the bombardment subsided, I climbed the final four steps and approached her bedroom door.

My stomach ached; saliva filled my mouth and cold sweat oozed down my back. I pushed open the door. Everything seemed normal. She was in bed.

'Where have you been? I'm dying of thirst.'

'Sorry Mother.' I set the tray on the bedside table. A thick, black photo album rested on her lap. What are you up to? I thought.

'Water bottle,' she demanded. There was no way I was giving him up this time. I needed Pooh if I was going to get through this. I clutched him tight to my chest; I could feel my skin reddening from the heat. 'I'm sorry ... it's still cold ... I forgot to refill it—'

'Oh, you really are hopeless—' She stopped herself and smiled. 'I don't know how you would survive without me telling you what to do. And I can't cope without you, Agnes.' Hell. She smiled at me and used my real name. What was she planning?

'Come sit with me.' She patted the bed. 'Look at this with me.' She opened the album and pointed at a faded image. 'That's Auntie Brenda.'

I felt weak but I remained standing. I had to tell her, no matter what she did to prevent me from going. If I did not face up to her this time, Pooh would never talk to me again. 'Mum ... I have to tell you something—'

'She loved her hats did your Auntie Brenda.'

'Mum, can you listen please?'

'We buried her in that hat.' She turned the page and pointed out another photo. 'That's your Uncle Geoffrey. Mad about motorcycles he was.'

'Mum, I'm leaving.' A deafening thump of thunder added a suitable full stop to my statement. She glanced at me.

'No, you're not,' she said softly. 'Poor old Geoffrey, I knew those bikes would be the death of him.'

'SOD BRENDA AND GEOFFREY, THEY'RE DEAD! I NEED A LIFE.'

'How dare you—'

'I'm forty-five, Mum. I want my own life. I want to get married. I want to have a baby. I want to do what I want to do.'

'You, have a baby?' she spluttered back. 'You're too old. Even if you did have one, you wouldn't last two minutes. You have enough trouble looking after yourself. And who would want to marry you, anyway?'

'Michael did!'

'Him? He was a waste of space.' The abrupt pelting of hailstones on the window startled both of us.

'I'm going,' I said in a calm voice. 'I'll arrange a home help for you.'

'So, this is it.' She looked at her photos. 'I'm to die alone.'

'What are you talking about? I'm not abandoning you. I just need to get my life sorted. I'll visit you.'

'No, you won't. Once you go you won't come back and I'll be on my own. Brenda left me. Geoffrey left me. Your dad left me. Now you're leaving me. I might as well die right now and save you the bother of walking out.'

Hugging her album, she rocked back and forth. It was unnerving to see her like this. Vulnerable.

'Go on then, if you're going,' she said.

I sat next to her and put a hand on her shoulder. 'It's ok; I'll pour you some tea. You'll feel better in a moment.'

'You are a good girl. Give your old mum a cuddle?'

I put Pooh down and hugged her.

'I've been a bad mother I know. You need to go and live a bit and I accept that. But, could you stay just one more night? Let me adjust?'

'Ok.'

She shifted position and a waft of lavender filled my nostrils and immediately began to suffocate me.

'No!' I leapt up snatching Pooh from her bed. 'I have to go now.' I ran from the room.

I had to side step down the stairs so that I did not fall. I could hear her getting out of bed. I reached the front door and fumbled with the latch until the door opened.

'Agony, if you go out that door I'll throw myself down these stairs and it will be your fault.'

She stood at the edge of the stairs, grasping her dreaded hand bell. An evil smirk spread across her face. I looked at her, then at the downpour outside.

'It'll be on your conscience if I die falling down the stairs.'

Mother's black silhouette flickered at the top of the stairs in the strobe light effect from multiple lightning flashes. The shadow of her outstretched arms jerked down the walls of the staircase in a creepy stop-motion fashion accompanied by a rolling crescendo of thunder. The black elongated shapes of her grasping fingers advanced to keep me ensnared.

I stepped into the freezing rain. Hailstones ricocheted off my thin body. I felt alive. I felt liberated.

'I'm proud of you,' said Pooh, still clutched in my hand.

'I'm free.'

The clamour of Mother's hand bell filtered through the storm. I turned and saw her small crumpled body at the foot of the stairs. An outstretched arm with an accusing finger pointed at me. Her eyes stared at me and I felt my hold on Pooh weaken. I wanted to turn my back on her. I wanted to walk away. But, I stood there. Staring. Waiting. The rain did its best to drown me for daring to leave. The wind blew around the corner of the house and I thought I heard a voice.

'Help me, Agony.'

'Honey pot, it's time to go.'

'Agony, help your old Mum.'

'Honey pot, come on. This is your chance.'

'Agnes, my sweet little girl. Please.'

I could not walk away and leave her laying there. My hot-water bottle fell to the ground and I returned to the house. I took Mother's outstretched hand and felt for a pulse. I could feel her lifeless eyes watching me. Judging me. The wind blew past the open front door, carrying a voice in the air.

'Useless girl.'

I picked up the phone in the hallway and dialled 999.

'Hello, police please. ... I have just killed my mother.'

FRAMED

T.R. Hitchman

It had been a good morning's work. John took a long, much needed intake of nicotine, and continued drawing on his hand-rolled cigarette till it burned dangerously close to his fingers. It hadn't been a particularly stressful morning, but it was his first cigarette since he had begun several hours ago – it didn't do to smoke whilst he was working – and he was missing the fix.

Sitting in his car, he chucked the dying cigarette stub out of the window, and surveyed the morning's takings – a wad of notes rolled up and banded tightly together with a thin brown sliver of rubber. He had been adding to it throughout the morning, but until now had resisted the urge to fan through them, to count them, to savour their feel – giving himself something to look forward to, like a child at Christmas. Eventually he couldn't resist any longer and spread them out on his lap. A mixture of twenties and tens, he picked them up, felt them between his fingers, and brought the notes up to his nostrils and inhaled deeply. It was as intoxicating as the nicotine had been, and he closed his eyes, losing himself in the moment, wondering if anything had smelt this good.

It had been a different story several months ago. Prison, the longest stretch so far, and he had walked out of the gates with nothing but the clothes he had been arrested in and a cheap canvas bag that was as empty of valuable contents as the pockets of his fraying overcoat. It made him sick even now to think of it. Walking out the gates, he'd looked back and had caught the screw giving him a wry smile that seemed to say *you'll be back*, and he had fought not to give the man a quick gesture with his finger. It had been March when he had been sent down and the cold, icy shiver that ran down his spine belied the promise of spring in the air and warm, lighter evenings. They would mean little to him inside. True, it was not the first time he had been detained at Her Majesty's pleasure, but this particular stretch had been the longest so far and it had felt like it every day. Perhaps he was getting too old for it. John had shared a cell with some elderly crim and had studied that toothless man with an equal measure of loathing and pity. He had studied too his own reflection, the sandy blond hair that was already getting thin on top, a once strong jaw now beginning to sag as time and his liking for a pint or two took their toll. Staring into the reflection of his own pale blue eyes, he imagined a much older man staring back at him with the backdrop of the same cell behind him.

And John had tried to go straight in the first month. Even attempted a bit of optimism at his first probation interview, trying his best to believe the woman behind the desk, nervously promising him through thin and insipid lips that she was sure that people 'would give him a chance' and that there was a very different attitude to ex-offenders in 'this day and age'. They found him a job of sorts in the end. Door-to-door salesman, selling cleaning products that nobody wanted to buy. Spending his days looking at shut doors and bored housewives who sneered 'that it was cheaper at that supermarket up the road anyway'. Waking up each morning with that sick feeling that began at the bottom of his stomach and by the time he had shut the front door had risen up to his throat and burned there for the rest of the day. It hadn't been the first time he had felt like this: it was the same back at school having to face those kids time and time again, but one day he had walked out of the gates of St Oswald's and had never looked back. This time he couldn't do the same; he was too old for running.

But then John got a chance. He'd been invited in by some old dear, who judging by the state of the hallway and the room he found himself being led into, hadn't used cleaning products for a good many years. John had sat dubiously on a dusty armchair and had waited whilst she crept despairingly slowly to the kitchen to make him a cup of tea. The drawer of a cupboard had been tantalisingly left half-open and he had instinctively pulled it open a little further, spotting the creased, brown envelope residing there. John had counted it when he had got back to his bedsit. Two hundred pounds. More than he had made in a couple of weeks. There in his hand, as easy as that. He had hidden it for a couple of days, a trick learned from his time inside, wrapped up in a couple of socks. Then he had waited for that knock on the door, for the police car to take him to the station. But nobody ever came. So, he had gone out with a couple of twenties and bought his first drink in weeks. It tasted good, that pint, and the whisky after that. It seemed that lady luck had finally decided that it was his turn.

John quickly learned that a wide smile and a bit of charm got him a lot. He still found it strangely alarming that these old dears would gladly invite him, a complete stranger, into their homes with only a scruffy laminated card to show them. Like a pig seeking out truffles, they seemed desperate for any kind of company and were all too willing to invite him in with the promise of few minutes of his time.

There had been only one moment when he had felt an uncomfortable twinge of guilt. The woman had appeared unexpectedly behind him, and in the struggle he had knocked her to the ground. Sometimes he still woke up in a sweat about her, wondering how long she was laid out on the floor, whether she ever got up again. He was glad to get shot of the ring he had stolen from her.

The jewellery had been an unexpected sideline. It took a bit more work – he had to be careful – but still a good few quid could be made from a gold bracelet, even a silver frame. John had got quite good at spotting the real thing and Google had been an invaluable teacher.

John started his car and began his drive home. The morning's haul put any thoughts of further work that day out of his mind. But then he drove past a house which had something about it that drew his eye to it. It was the oldest one by far on the street, looking out of place, like a rotten tooth. There were more modern buildings in the street that perhaps would have held the promise of richer pickings, but there was something about the decaying grandeur of the old house, like the faded elegance of a woman who though past her best still had some essence of her glamorous youth. He parked the car a street away and had taken a leisurely walk back to the old house.

The gate had seen better days too. John had to use a little more force than was good for it to push it open, and he left it dangling precariously on its one remaining hinge. The front garden was a mass of weed and overgrown grass. John could just about make out the path, and at one point as he made his way to the front door he snagged his trousers on an overgrown hawthorn bush. The door hinted at its ostentatious past, but years of neglect had left it a shadow of its former self. Now, paint peeled away like torn skin, exposing the woodwork beneath, and rust had bloomed on the ornate knocker that John, against his better judgement, began to rap the door with.

John waited, fighting against his impatience which gnawed away at him like a hunger. It took them time; he often would imagine the laborious journey they would make from their armchair, to the hallway and then the door itself. Gradually the blurred outline in the frosted glass. There was no glass to peer through this time, but he heard the chorus of bolts being unlocked, and gradually the door was eased open.

John studied the woman who stood blinking in the sunlight. About half his height and bent over, she peered up at him behind a pair of glasses whose style had long gone out of fashion.

'Good afternoon.' The woman continued to stare. John took a confident step forward. There was a technique to this. John had perfected it over the past few months. It was never good to be too pushy at first; like a child he would initially stand a few paces back, as if he was the one who should be cautious. There was certainly no place for that cocky attitude he had picked up during his years spent at Her Majesty's pleasure. John gave it a few moments, before he gradually moved a couple more steps forward.

'I'm sorry to trouble you, but wonder if I could interest you in a few products that I'm trying to sell?' The woman continued to stare, her milky blue eyes taking him in. John felt he was being studied, as if she were a painter taking in the details of her subject before putting brush to canvas.

'You said that before, Simon. You know you're not, you

silly boy. Come on now, that tap of mine is still leaking; you promised to fix it.' She opened the door wider then, smiling at the face she thought she recognised. John grinned too.

'Of course, my memory must be getting bad. Yep, let's have a look at this tap of yours.' Chuckling as he walked inside, he couldn't believe his luck.

The woman had taken such small dawdling steps, making her way around the piles of papers and books that littered the hallway, making it like an obstacle course. Every muscle in John's legs ached with impatience, and he fought the urge to push her forward. Eventually he was led into a room and he entered it with an unusual caution.

At first it almost took his breath away. On every available surface, whether it was a shelf, a table or a bookcase, were frames of various shapes and styles. Some were perched on the very edge of the mantelpiece Many were stacked side by side, a continuous snake which seemingly had no end. The effect was so claustrophobic that John struggled for air.

'Jesus Christ, you know a lot of people...' John joked without smiling. He turned to catch the woman grinning childishly at him.

'Oh Simon, you said that last time too. Your memory, it's as bad as mine.' She gripped his arm tightly, and John had the urge to shake off the claw-like grip. 'Now, you stay here while I get that cup of tea. Don't you run off like you did last time. Think I've got a biscuit too, know how you boys love those.' She giggled, the face wrinkling up in a perverted kind of delight, the expression not quite right on a woman of her years.

It was as if everybody she had ever known was captured. Now left on his own, John couldn't help but study the photographs that were littered everywhere. He picked one up, quickly glancing at the person staring back at him, but turned it around and smiled when he found the desired hallmark. Real silver. It was small, small enough for it to be slipped into his jacket pocket and John did it instinctively. He scanned the room; there were probably more frames with a value to be found in amongst the multitude. He'd got to know a jeweller in town, a backstreet place; they didn't ask too many questions. He could get a few quid for some good quality frames there.

John was suddenly drawn to an old-fashioned style bureau at the end of the room, the sort that people used to use to write letters; he'd seen one like it on one of his Google searches. As he supposed it might be, it was unlocked and he pulled the lid down carefully. He began to work quickly. John had eagerly spied an old trinket box in the corner and had pulled it out, but it contained merely worthless costume jewellery; that was no good at all. Chains now tinged with green, a ring with several of its gaudy glass stones missing. John threw the box back in with frustration, and without thinking slammed the lid down so hard that a couple of the frames that were balanced on top toppled to the floor.

The fall smashed the glass of one of them. John picked it up, trying his best not to cut his fingers on the shards that littered the carpet. The frame itself was cheap, the sort you'd buy in those tacky gift shops in town, and he was about to hide its remains in the bureau when the photograph caught his eye. A young girl, standing proud, or so it seemed, perhaps on her first day at school. He recalled his mum capturing a similar image with her cheap little camera, hauled out for special occasions. He suddenly remembered a photograph somewhere, his hair wonkily cut, that blazer a bit too big, his hands disappearing up the sleeves like a magician's. But as John looked closer, he realised that the girl wasn't smiling. Her hands were clasped together, as if she were praying, and the face wore an expression of fear. It almost looked as though she was pleading with whoever was taking the photograph. It gave him a funny feeling and he placed it face down; though the image remained in his head for a while.

John began to look at the other photographs now. Faces, stiff and frightened, glared accusingly back at him. Strange, but none of them were smiling. They all wore that peculiar expression, the same look, the men restraining from showing it too much, the women unable to pretend. It was the eyes, looking at John, pleading with him – or so it seemed in this particular minute – to be released from their prison of glass and photographic paper. There was one that caught his eye; though black and white, as they all were, there was something very modern about the uniform the man in it was wearing, overalls, as if he worked for some kind of maintenance company, the sort of bloke he spotted every day going about their business. And his face – this particular image was blurred, but as John peered closely he could see that the man had his mouth opened wide, eyes shut, as if he were screaming.

'Now that's Philip. I thought he was a nice lad.' John had been so engrossed that he hadn't realised that the old woman was standing behind him. Like a cat, she had crept up on him. She was smiling, and there was something very feline in the way her lips curled over her teeth, her eyes peering into his own with a kind of malice. He began to back away a little, and winced when he felt the crunch of broken glass beneath his feet.

'I wasn't nicking anything, I... I was just looking at the photographs.' In that moment John suddenly remembered the first time he got caught. Barely fifteen, he'd done it to impress some older boys. There was that long ride home in the police car, him squirming in the back seat whilst that red-faced policeman glared at him from the front. And then his mum's face at the door, the sound of her crying and Dad's footsteps on the stairs, the belt being tightened in his hands.

'He came to fix my boiler, lovely young man, not like you, Simon; you're a very naughty boy, aren't you?'

John looked desperately over her shoulder. It would be easy, just give her a push, a little one; she'd be on the floor, squirming like a wasp on its back, and he'd be out of that door in no time.

But he couldn't move. Transfixed, his feet seemingly refusing to budge, his skin glistening with a layer of cold, clammy perspiration. John had dealt with worse than this in prison; he had had his run-ins with many a fellow inmate who wanted to show him who was boss. His dad was no pushover either. But this old woman, there was something about the way she grinned inanely at him, the smell of her, the crackle of static as the arms of her cardigan rubbed against her body. And she was holding something behind her back, trying her best to conceal whatever it was and that she was itching to reveal.

She seemed to be addressing somebody else in the room, raising her voice a little as if they sat in the corner.

'And you're going to stay with us, aren't you? Yes, Simon, you're not going anywhere.' She gave a childish giggle at the end, smiling, creeping towards him. And then he saw what she had in her hand. A camera, an old box brownie, battered around the edges, bits of brown leather peeling away. She waved it at him and he stared at it confused. 'Come on, Simon, don't be shy...' She pointed it towards him then.

He saw them in the lens then. All of them. The schoolgirl, the young man who had come only to fix the boiler, women, children, men, all screaming, pleading to be released, but instead the flash and then they were imprisoned, trapped behind the glass. She collected them, a lepidopterist collecting her butterflies, and then displaying them in this room.

John held his hand up, but the bright light of the flash seeped through the gaps of his fingers and he shut his eyes to protect them.

'Smile for the camera, dear.'

A HEALTH AND SAFETY ISSUE

Rosemary Salter

I don't know where to start, Inspector, it's been a helluva shock to us all. You don't expect this sort of thing to happen in a *tax office*. I mean, it's supposed to be boring and uneventful and it is, most of the time, but *now!* Roger's so *ordinary*, never hurt a fly – well, at least, not unless it was eating his precious plants! Sorry, I didn't mean to be facetious, it's just so hard to take in...

What? Start at the beginning? Well, I joined the happy band about eighteen months ago. It wasn't the career I had envisaged when I left Uni, to be honest, but needs must and it was the only place that offered me a half-decent position. When I arrived, I was surprised that there were just four of us: I'd imagined a large open plan area full of clerks in grey suits beavering away without talking to each other. But it wasn't like that. There were only a few of us, as I say – a rather specialised field, you understand – and the others were a pleasant surprise as well.

Jim had been there five or six years. He was the joker, always quick with a quip to lighten the most mundane task. Madeleine was the sole woman, middle-aged, but still trim if you catch my drift, and with a sense of humour, too – she could hold her own when the jokes became a bit ribald.

Then there was Roger. Roger was more your typical civil servant, in his fifties, neatly cut hair, always wore a tie. He'd been in the forces, I gathered, and when he'd done his stint, he became a public servant out of choice rather than necessity or lethargy like the rest of us. He kept his head down and got on with his work. Not that he wasn't friendly, he was just quiet and conscientious.

You're recording all this, aren't you, Inspector? It's important for you to know the background and to understand the personalities involved in this – awful *thing* that's happened.

Roger didn't make much of an impression on me at first; our conversation was limited to 'good morning', 'good night' and very little in between – but, after I'd been there a week or two, I saw a different side to him. You see, Roger had a hobby – no, passion is a better word – his garden. All Jim had to do was ask casually how his weekend had been and he'd be away, telling you how tall his sweet peas were growing and how he was hoping to enter his dahlias in the local show. I think Jim used to set him off deliberately sometimes, if he fancied a break from whatever he was doing. He didn't do it unkindly, mind – we all liked Roger, even if he was easy to tease. Apparently, he'd always enjoyed gardening, but after his wife passed on a couple of years ago it became almost an obsession, something to fill the long, lonely hours outside work, I guess. And it wasn't only flowers. Oh no, he grew a wide variety of veg and he was proud of his 'mini orchard' as he called it; he was looking forward to picking his plums and damsons. He didn't keep them to himself, either; he was generous like that, often bringing in courgettes or tomatoes to share round.

No, Inspector, I'm not rambling. You'll see my point in due course.

As I said, when I arrived, that made up the complement of four admin officers. We were lacking a supervisor – the last one had gone on maternity leave and had recently announced that she was not intending to return. Madeleine, by virtue of her length of service, had been acting up for three months, had done a reasonable job according to Jim and now, not unreasonably, was expecting her temporary promotion to become permanent. Alas, things do not work that way in Her Majesty's Revenue and Customs, and soon a rumour reached the collective ears of our little department that a new person, gender, age and name as yet unknown, was to be parachuted in over Madeleine – and the rest of us, of course.

Julia – Mrs Garvey – duly took up her post. A period of adjustment, on both sides, followed. She'd come from another area, somewhere down south I think, and had rather fixed ideas about how things should be run. I'd simply gone along with the pattern established by the others under their previous manager and continued during her absence. It was pretty laid back but the job got done. The atmosphere changed with Julia's arrival. It became less relaxed, less convivial, more *business-like*, I suppose you'd describe it. She made it clear, not through anything she said but by a certain look she had, that she disapproved of Jim's particular brand of humour. He toned it down. We came to a slightly uneasy compromise over working practices; we accepted that she was a new broom wanting to make her mark. She'd probably mellow.

Don't get me wrong, Inspector, none of us disliked Julia. No, as a person she was nice enough. It's difficult for anyone to come into a close-knit environment and attempt to introduce their own methods, and Julia had the added disadvantage of having to find her feet in a strange part of the country. It doesn't matter what anyone says, there is still a north-south divide and ways of operating in the 'soft south' are quite different from the down-to-earth north – or, at least, that's how we saw it.

Take her preoccupation with health and safety, for instance. She hadn't been here a fortnight before she carried out a risk assessment. We'd been accustomed to propping open the fire door which led from the main office into the tiny kitchen, so much easier when you were going backwards and forwards carrying cups of coffee. Julia put a stop to this and insisted that, inconveniently, the door must remain closed at all times. There again, we were perfectly happy to squash into the broom cupboard that housed the photocopier, ignoring the heat and lack of air as we reeled off dozens of copies. Julia was appalled and immediately ordered the copier to be brought out of the cupboard and placed in the corner where, hitherto, we had dumped our bags and briefcases and coats. Oh, and the microwave vanished. We could hardly complain about that – it wasn't exactly the latest model and the sparks that flew whenever it was switched on were a little disconcerting.

And then there were the signs. A freshly-typed plan of what to do in event of a fire or other emergency was stuck up in a prominent position and a laminated, up to date, version of the Health and Safety at Work Act made its appearance on the noticeboard, replacing the dog-eared A2 sheet that had been there for as long as even Madeleine could remember. That was fair enough, we conceded; perhaps we had been a bit lackadaisical about safety issues. But then notices began to pop up all over the place – in the kitchen, telling us to be sure to wash out our mugs

PROPERLY so as not to spread germs and warning that the water from the hot water tap was, well, hot; in the toilets, reminding us to wash our hands. Above each workstation was fixed a card saying THINK BEFORE YOU DRINK – SPILLS CAUSE BREAKDOWNS.

We laughed about it at first; this zeal would wear off when she was settled in. But it didn't.

Yes, yes, Inspector, I thought you wanted to find out what might have led up to this – dreadful *thing* that's happened?

On the whole, we were a contented group, despite Julia's foibles, and we regarded each other as friends as well as colleagues. We shared both joyful and sad occasions. One of our traditions was the celebration of a birthday by the lucky person baking, if they were capable, buying if they weren't, a selection of cakes, in exchange for a card purchased from the cheap stall in the market and signed by everyone. A couple of months after Julia's arrival, it happened to be Madeleine's *special* birthday and she had really gone to town with the cakes. A tin full of muffins and scones and a delicious Victoria sponge was sitting on the shelf in the kitchen at coffee break. We tried our best to polish them off but failed, so we left the rest to enjoy the next day. When 11 o'clock came round the following morning, neither cakes nor tin were anywhere to be seen. Odd, we thought, perhaps Madeleine had changed her mind and taken them home with her. But no, she was as mystified as the rest of us. We only solved the mystery when Julia said, almost as an aside: 'Oh, I'm sorry, Madeleine, I had to throw out the cakes, the tin was rusty and it could have given us food poisoning.'

Then there was the incident of the yoghurts – I'm building up a picture of how it was, Inspector, of a possible explanation for this – what's happened. Jim was on one of his periodic diets – or, more accurately, Jim's *wife* was on a diet and Jim had the choice of participating or getting his own meals. Instead of his usual doorstep sandwich, packet of crisps and hunk of cake, it was a green salad, an apple and a yoghurt for lunch. Well, now and again, Jim succumbed to temptation and sneaked out to buy a doughnut or a bar of chocolate – he looked guilty, mind, to be fair. Consequently, the family-size box of yoghurts took a while to diminish. This did not worry Jim in the slightest. *It's full of bacteria, anyway*, he'd say cheerfully. It obviously worried someone else, though. One lunchtime, Jim went in search of a black cherry, his favourite, to find the fridge empty apart from a pint of milk. Julia's comment when confronted? 'They were two days past their best before date. I can't risk my staff going down with botulism!'

Well, Jim held back a retort – Julia was his boss, after all – but, once she was out of earshot, he let rip to the rest of us: 'It's health and safety gone mad, that's what it is! Who does she think she is, throwing away perfectly good food, *our* food! I haven't forgotten your cakes, Madeleine!'

Madeleine joined in. 'Don't get me started! It's the notices and petty rules I resent. Treating us as if we were kids!'

Roger said nothing, he just shrugged and carried on with his spreadsheet.

After that, we were careful not to leave anything around that Julia might take exception to. When Roger brought in jars of home-made courgette and apple chutney, even a small one for Julia, we took it home rather than eat it at work. But you forget, don't you, and things soon returned to what passed for normality in a tax office.

You needn't glance at your watch, Inspector, I'm up to recent events now.

Last weekend, not this Saturday gone, the one before, the annual local produce show was held in the community centre. Roger had been telling us what classes he planned to enter. He was so dedicated to his gardening that we weren't a bit surprised when he won a silver and gold for his roses and dahlias as well as second prize for his plum jam, first for his chutney and first PLUS a special award for his damson wine! He was thrilled to bits, so proud, especially since he'd dipped his toe into wine-making only last autumn. On Friday he brought in a bottle for us to sample. I didn't need to have tasted any of the other entries to know that, indisputably, the judges had made the right decision. Even Julia said how delicious it was. Of course, she had to go and spoil it by commenting on how *potent* it was also. She insisted that a small glass was quite enough – in case of accidents involving machinery... 'Drunk in charge of a keyboard,' Madeleine muttered. 'You couldn't make it up!'

I assumed that Roger would take home the remains of the wine, but obviously he didn't because when I came in on Monday morning – yesterday, it seems an age ago – I wandered into the kitchen to make a brew to find him staring disconsolately at an empty bottle. 'Been at the drink already, Rog?' I joked. He turned to me with an odd expression on his face. 'She's poured it away, down the sink, *my* wine, *my prize-winning* wine.'

I did not need to ask who 'she' was. Roger seemed incapable of moving, so I took it upon myself to march into her office to express righteous indignation on his behalf.

'You can't leave home-made wine once it's been opened,' she said. 'I'm sorry if Roger's upset but it's a matter of health and safety. He can do what he likes at home but here staff welfare is my responsibility. Now, if that's all, I suggest we get on with our work.'

What could I say? Madeleine and Jim were equally annoyed but, at the end of the day, we were employees and had to do as we were told. The only way we could express our feelings was by not speaking to Julia unless it was unavoidable. Roger put his head down and applied himself to a complex report.

He hadn't quite finished it by five, so Jim, Madeleine and I left him to it. Julia was still there; she was always the last to leave.

I was the first to arrive this morning and, as per normal, before I even switched on my computer, breezed into the kitchen in search of coffee to wake me up. While I was standing by the sink waiting for the kettle to boil, I became aware of a funny smell. I couldn't identify it. It was a sort of sweet and sour smell. Into my head, goodness knows why, popped the aroma of last night's steak – before it was cooked. I sniffed my way round the kitchen trying to find the source. On the draining board were a few spots of what looked like rust. Perhaps we needed to buy a new kettle. There was no point checking the fridge: there'd be nothing gone off in there, thanks to Julia's diligence.

I shrugged and walked back into the main office to open a window to let in a bit of fresh air. Then I saw a strange thing – the filing cabinet in the corner had three of its four drawers stuck out. Now, it was one of Julia's strictest rules that only one drawer at a time should be pulled out in case the whole thing toppled forward and squashed the unfortunate person doing the pulling. I went to push in the drawers tidily before Julia arrived and jumped to the conclusion that I was the culprit. The top one was out the furthest and I gave it a shove. It didn't budge. It was jammed somehow. I peered inside but couldn't see anything apart from the rows of manila files sandwiched between dark green cardboard dividers. I felt around right at the back. My fingers touched something soft yet firm. What the..? I wiggled the object and managed to extricate it.

It was a foot. It was encased in a maroon and cream striped sock and attached to an ankle. I gave a shriek and dropped it. It landed between sections D and E, as I recall. I slammed the drawer shut. As I did so, the drawer below revealed its contents – the pair to the foot, the matching lower legs (in black trousers) and two folded arms draped in a red silky material. I yelled and ran across the room as far as I could go. At that moment, Madeleine and Jim turned up. I gabbled at them and gesticulated wildly at the filing cabinet.

We approached, Madeleine and Jim curiously, me reluctantly.

While I was fetching a glass of water to revive Madeleine, Jim gingerly inspected the third and fourth drawers.

'You don't want to see what's in there', he said, sombrely.

It was then I noticed the neat pile of files stacked on a chair next to the filing cabinet. And on top lay a knife. It was the sharp knife we used to slice birthday cakes. Tied to its shaft was a piece of card. Jim, who seemed to be the least squeamish of the three of us, took out his handkerchief and caught hold of it to examine it more closely. 'It's a label,' he exclaimed, 'the sort of label that you tie to plants and shrubs and such-like. And there's writing on it.'

'What does it say?'

'SHARP KNIVES SHOULD NOT BE ALLOWED IN THE WORKPLACE. THEY'RE A HEALTH AND SAFETY HAZARD.'

BAD BOYS DON'T GET DESSERT

William Quincy Belle

Henry stood in front of a wall-mounted case containing small plastic drawers. Dad said he had taken possession of the case when a local dentist had given up his practice and sold all the office furniture and professional equipment. The drawers made for a great organizational tool in the basement workshop. His dad had labeled each drawer with magic marker and filled them all with various items like nails, screws, Marr connectors, and what-have-you. Henry was now scanning each row, looking for something specific. Third row, second drawer from the left: razor blades. Dad always used a razor to shave and kept the discarded blades in case he needed to do some precision cutting.

Henry pulled the drawer open, examining the scattered pile of half a dozen blades. He picked up the top blade with his thumb and index finger. Shutting the drawer, Henry held up the blade. This was perfect; it would do the job nicely.

He turned around and faced the terrified man, held captive in a wooden chair. He was wide-eyed and breathing heavily through his nose, mouth stuffed with a ball gag. Henry's prisoner was bathed in sweat.

'When I was six, Dad showed me an old black-and-white silent film called *An Andalusian Dog*. It was one of the first surrealist films.' Henry turned the blade around between his fingers. 'I was fascinated by the opening scene, where the filmmaker slits a woman's eye. Even though it was all fake – it was actually a calf's eye – it was powerful, horrifying. There are things that get you right in the gut. What's the word?' Henry looked away and furrowed his brow. 'Visceral.' He gave the man a triumphant look. 'That's it, "visceral".'

Henry stepped forward and walked around the chair. 'Last year I dissected a cow's eye in biology class and that was sort of the same thing, but it wasn't a human eye.' He took up position behind the man. 'I thought since you were here, I should take advantage of the opportunity.'

Henry grabbed the man's forehead with his left hand and brought his right, which held the razor, to the man's face. The man tried to scream, but the ball gag muffled any sound. He tried to twist in the chair but was firmly bound in place.

The man went suddenly limp. Henry stopped and let go of the man's head, watching it flop forward onto his chest. The man had fainted. No matter, this would make things easier.

Supporting the man's head with his left hand, Henry used his thumb and index finger to pry apart one eyelid. The eye had rolled back in the head, so the white was almost completely exposed. Henry leaned over as he brought the razor up, then, using the sharp point, sliced into the eyeball from left to right. The clear gel of the interior of the eye, the vitreous humor, spilled out. Henry looked at it curiously, touching the substance with the end of his index finger. Using his left hand, he squeezed the eyelids together, trying to coax the remnants of the gel out. He looked again at the substance, trying to remember what it had looked like in the movie. How strange, and yet how similar.

'Henry!' His mother's disembodied voice came from the top of the stairs.

Letting go of the man's head, Henry stood up straight. 'Yes, Mom?' He remained still, straining to hear.

'Dinner!'

'Okay, Mom. I'll be right up.'

He walked across to the workbench, leaving the razor blade before heading to the stairs. Henry flicked off the light and headed up to the kitchen, where his mother was busy serving up two plates.

'Wash your hands, dear.'

'Yes, ma'am. What's for dinner?'

'I had to stay a little late at the store tonight, so I didn't have a lot of time to do much. Fortunately, I did have frozen pork chops. I hope you don't mind, dear.'

Henry walked back into the kitchen and sat down. 'Mom, come on. You know I love your cooking. Even when you're not trying, you make something tasty. I hope I can develop the same skill — to create something from nothing.'

She laughed as she set two plates on the table. 'Well, aren't you the charmer. Certainly, your father never complained.' His mother paused, then said 'Bless his soul.' She crossed herself before turning back to the stove and fiddling with the burner controls. She remained there, standing still with her back to Henry, but her sniffling told him she was on the verge of crying.

'I miss him, too.' Henry tried to change the subject. 'I'm starving. And you must be, too. You were saying you had a longer day than normal?'

'Yes.' She took out a tissue and blew her nose. 'Let's eat.' She sat down and smiled at her son.

Henry stared at his plate. 'Ooh, baked potato.' He reached over, pulled the butter dish closer to his plate, and cut the potato into smaller chunks.

'Your Aunt Teresa's coming over tonight after dinner.' His mom pointed to a white cardboard box on the counter. 'By the way, I picked us up a treat; your favorite, in fact.'

'You mean ...?'

'Yes, Boston cream pie.'

Henry was both surprised and pleased.

'Aunt Teresa and I are planning the church picnic.'

'Oh?'

'Yes. A week from this Sunday. We're going to have a church social after the 11 a.m. service. Teresa and I are heading up the women's group to arrange a picnic brunch. I hope you'll come.'

'Of course I will. I can help out with the tables and chairs. I'm sure you could use an extra pair of hands.' Henry spread chunks of butter over the pieces of potato. 'Oh, I love a baked potato with butter.'

'I'd appreciate it. We'd all appreciate it.' She put a piece of pork in her mouth and chewed.

Henry scooped up some potato and had raised his fork about halfway to his mouth when a blood-curdling scream erupted from the basement. He froze and stared at his mother. For a few silent moments, she stared back at him, wide-eyed.

'Henry, what was that?'

There was another scream.

'Good lord! What in heaven's name is going on?' She immediately pushed her chair back and stood up.

'Mom, I can explain ...' But his mother had already headed for the basement and Henry ran after her.

Storming down the basement steps, Henry's mother turned on the light. The sound of sobbing came from the workshop. She marched across the open area, turned the corner and came to a dead halt in front of the man in the chair. 'Oh ... my ... God ...!'

Henry came up behind his mother. 'Mom, I can explain ...'

She turned around to face her son, furious. 'Henry! How many times have I told you to not do this in the house?'

'I ...'

'You're supposed to do this in the shed. If your father were alive, he'd tan your hide.' She crossed herself again and looked at the ceiling. 'Bless his soul.'

'But I put down a tarp.'

She turned back to face the man. He whimpered, staring at her with his right eye; his left eyelid had caved into the socket.

'Look at this mess,' she said. 'Your father always kept a neat workshop and – here, look at what you've done! My God, you've got blood on the floor!' She pointed to the floor around the chair. 'You're going to clean that up, young man. You'll respect the memory of your dead father by respecting his workshop.'

Henry stood with his shoulders and head lowered, looking at his feet. 'Yes, ma'am.'

'Your father always told you to keep the hobbies out back in the shed. That's what it's there for. It's far easier to hose down the shed than try to keep the workshop clean. Heck, you start sawing through a body and you end up with blood and flesh everywhere. It's a nightmare to clean up, and if you don't do it properly, that stuff starts to stink after a while.'

'Yes, ma'am.'

Henry's mother turned back to stare at the captive. She stepped forward and leaned over to look at his hands. 'What's this?' She pointed at the right hand, palm down on the wooden armrest. Two metallic spots could be seen protruding through the back of his hand.

'Uh ... galvanized plasterboard nails.'

She nodded, half-smiling. 'Very good. I'm impressed.' She looked at the left hand, discovering the same thing. He had first strapped the man's wrists to the armchair, then hammered two large nails through the back of each hand to secure it to the arm. Henry's captive couldn't move his hands without further ripping his flesh.

'Let's see; fingernails ripped out, the little finger amputated.' His mother nodded as she looked over the man. 'Very good.'

Henry grinned. 'Thanks, I ...'

'Henry?' She continued to study the man.

He stopped mid-sentence.

'Please don't do this again.'

'Yes, ma'am.'

'I want you to use the shed.'

'Yes, ma'am.'

She looked at the man's left eye, leaning in to get a closer look. 'What did you do to the eye?'

'I ...' Henry shifted on the balls of his feet. 'I slit it open with a razor blade.'

His mother clicked her tongue and shook her head. 'You and your father and that Dali film. Geesh, you both seem to be obsessed with eyeballs.'

The captive stared at her with his one good eye, saliva

dribbling from his mouth. His voice was almost a whisper. 'Help me.'

Henry's mother looked the man in his good eye. She held his gaze and said 'Aunt Teresa will be here at seven and I don't want her to have to put up with any screaming from the basement. We've important things to discuss and I don't want any interruptions.'

'I don't know how he got the ball gag out of his mouth.'

She sighed and straightened up, shaking her head. 'You're just like your father. He never did get the hang of securing a ball gag. I can't tell you how many times somebody cleared their mouth without using their hands.'

She walked over to one side of the workbench, opening the doors to the large wall-mounted cupboard. She looked around a moment before selecting something he couldn't see. Henry watched his mother turn back with a hatchet.

'Uh, Mom ...'

'I'm sorry, but you should know better. You have to suffer the consequences.'

She swung the hatchet in a large arc over her shoulder. The man gasped just before the blade sliced into the top of the head; Henry heard a heavy thump followed by a squishing sound. The man's body went rigid as his limbs spasmed. There was a whoosh as the air was expelled from his lungs and his head sank forward.

Henry and his mother looked at the man's skull, split open by the force of the blow. The hatchet was embedded in the flesh, but as they watched, it slowly tipped forward and fell onto the floor with a clatter.

'Henry?'

'Yes, ma'am.'

'You're not getting any dessert.'

'Aw, Mom ...'

She looked at her son with slight disdain. 'Don't you "Aw, Mom" me.' She pointed to the dead man. 'Get all of this cleaned up. I want that body outside immediately. You get it down to the wood chipper and mulch it before you come back in the house. And you're getting up early tomorrow morning to fertilize the back garden before you go to school.'

Henry muttered under his breath, 'Oh boy.'

'Pardon me?' She looked at him sternly.

'Nothing.'

'Now get busy.' She stood there, tapping her foot.

He sighed, walked over to the workbench. Picking up a hammer, he began removing the plasterboard nails with the claw.

'I'll keep your dinner warm.' She turned around and headed for the stairs. 'And I'll save you a piece of pie.'

Henry grinned. He knew she couldn't stay angry with him.

THE CASTLE OF LUNE

Philip Onions

On midsummer's eve, the tiny car left the hubbub of the city. It drove on through unfamiliar country roads. The further it went, the quieter the roads became and the narrower and more winding.

'For God's sake, cheer up, Lily,' Mallory White, the driver of the car, said to her daughter who was on the backseat behind her.

Lily stared sullenly out through the open window, her long, blond hair flapping around her head. She grunted in response to her mother.

'Sarah's your age, maybe you can become friends.'

Lily made no reply.

'Look, dear, I know this is all different for you, but this is really important to me. I need you to make a good impression on Lord Morgan when you meet him.' Mallory caught sight of Lily in the mirror rolling her eyes. 'Please...'

'Why?' Lily snapped back suddenly. 'I was happy! We were happy! Why d'you have to leave Dad? I don't want to live in a castle! I want to go back to the way things were. I want to go home!' After this outburst, Lily sat back furiously in her seat, crossed her arms and resumed her staring out the window at the countryside flashing by.

'I need this. I have to make a good impression,' Mallory said quietly.

'Well I don't!' Lily snapped back.

'No, you don't,' Mallory agreed. 'But if you promise to be back by eight, I don't mind if you and Sarah go off and play. But stay out of the forest.'

'Play? PLAY!' Lily snarled, and then rubbed the growing ache in her belly.

Mallory watched her daughter through the mirror as they drove on in silence.

The Castle of Lune was an imposing Gothic monstrosity, arrogantly thrusting skyward through the ancient parkland to make a bold statement as to the power and wealth of its original owners. The stonework was etched by the weather and ivy covered its walls. The windows were black, like soulless eyes staring out from a corpse's face. Lily shivered. A flock of jackdaws cawed and screeched as they wheeled about in the tower.

Lord Morgan was there to greet them, standing outside his castle. Despite his age, he was standing straight and tall. A strangely hypnotic twinkle emanated from his grey eyes as he watched Mallory and Lily White arrive. A dapper figure, he was dressed, as always for him, in an ensemble that included a waistcoat, cravat and, drooping from the top pocket of his jacket, a spotted handkerchief. He greeted each of his guests with charm and courtesy. When it was Lily's turn, he took her little hand in his and smiled deeply into her eyes.

'Hello, Lily White. What a lovely name. I have been so looking forward to meeting you and may I say how appropriate the name for such a pretty young lady.' His eyes seemed to bore deeply into her very soul; she could not turn away. Then, with a slight smile, as though he had read her inner thoughts, he continued in a whisper, 'I know you didn't want to come, but I hope you like it now that you're here.'

Lily blushed and looked at her shiny shoes.

'Is Sarah here?' Mallory asked, looking around. 'I thought she and Lily could go and explore the grounds, if you don't mind, my Lord?' she did an awkward, half curtsy, but Lord Morgan didn't seem to notice her clumsy effort.

'Oh yes, of course. I hope she and Lily will become great friends. They can explore the grounds, and take Alex with them, Sarah's older sister, just to keep them out of trouble. Now, where is she? Alex? Alex? Ah, there you are, could you be a dear and take Lily to find Sarah and go with them?'

Alex frowned, she didn't want to babysit the younger girls. She was tall for her age and wiry, more of a tomboy than Sarah or Lily. Her hair was short, her arms toned and she was wearing jeans and a T-shirt, not a summer frock. She rolled her eyes and looked at Morgan, but she knew better than to argue and, with a shrug, led Lily away to find Sarah.

'But stay out of the forest!' Lord Morgan called after them.

Defiantly, Lily led the others straight to the forest.

'But stay out of the forest!' Lily mimicked Lord Morgan's voice.

Throughout the forest, and since dawn, birds had been singing out as loudly as they could, defining their territory, calling for a mate and advising others to stay away; but as the humans crashed into their world, the birds in the forest fell silent.

'He gives me the creeps!' Lily laughed. 'Isn't he like Lord Voldemort?'

'He's got more hair! He's more like Saruman!' Sarah replied.

'Yeah, from *Lord of the Rings*!' Lily laughed.

Alex followed a little behind the younger girls. She walked with long, slow, sulky, deliberate strides, taking her time and dragging long grass stalks that she plucked at random as she watched the girls enjoy themselves.

The party made its way deeper into the forest. At one point Alex lost sight of Sarah and Lily – it seemed they resented her presence, feeling they didn't need her to be around to look after them. When she found them, they were in a more subdued mood than when she had lost them. They were now quite deep in the forest, and in the darkness and shadows it was unsettling for the younger girls. Alex found them with Lily sitting on a mossy rock massaging her stomach and Sarah standing over her new friend, her hand on Lily's shoulder.

'You okay?' Alex asked.

'Yeah.' Lily got up and kicked a nearby toadstool, part of a circle, then set off into the forest again with Sarah. Alex walked after them.

High above them, a pigeon suddenly exploded noisily out of the branches. The girls froze. They looked slowly about themselves, startled by the sudden noise.

'I don't like it, Sarah,' Lily said quietly. If the truth were told, Sarah wasn't too happy anymore either. She reached out her hand and took Lily's in hers. The two children looked at each other.

'Look it's okay,' Sarah said reassuringly. 'It was only a pigeon. I bet he was more scared of us than we were of him. Come on.'

Alex came up the path behind them. She seemed unconcerned by the sudden noise and the girls felt safer.

Hand in hand, they carried on down the steep, narrow woodland path, deeper into the forest.

They followed a track that descended a hill and were surprised to find at the end of it a small, weed-infested clearing, surrounded by an old, dilapidated fence. Two old horses were standing in the shade of an old oak on the far side of the meadow, head to tail, listlessly flicking the flies away from each other's faces. Beyond them was a derelict old cottage with a ramshackle barn built onto it, covered in ivy and with a large elderberry tree growing out the collapsed roof. It all looked as if the forest were reabsorbing it back into its wild state.

'Look at them,' Sarah whispered, pointing to the two old horses. 'Aren't they lovely?'

'Oh yes,' Lily agreed. 'How sweet, they're sniffing each other's bums!'

The girls stifled their giggles.

Alex walked up beside them. 'We should leave them alone; this place gives me the creeps.'

Sarah scowled at her sister.

'Let's go around there,' Sarah replied, rolling her eyes; and, pulling Lily after her, she set off through the trees, making her way around the clearing without waiting for Lily to reply.

'Sarah, wait!' Alex whispered urgently, but Sarah was not for waiting, nor heeding her older sister. She pushed on through the thick brambles at the edge of the meadow, rather than go out into the open, where she might have been seen. A small piece of her summer frock snagged on the thorns and she tugged at it to free it, ripping a small piece from the hem.

Alex followed them reluctantly, carefully picking the briars out of her path with her forefinger and thumb.

'Sarah! I don't like this! Come back.'

They approached the horses slowly from the forest edge. The one facing them looked around at the girl's approach, but the other was not bothered; it was too hot.

'Oh you're beautiful,' Lily said, reaching out to the mare. 'Do you think we could ride them?'

'No,' Alex replied urgently. 'They're too old! You don't know if they're broken in or wild!'

But Sarah ignored her and was already climbing the wooden fence next to the nearest.

'See! It's fine!' Sarah snapped at Alex. 'They might be old, but they're strong!'

'Get down!' Alex snapped back. 'It's not fair; it's too hot for them to be ridden!'

'Can I get up as well?' Lily asked in a whisper, making towards the fence.

'No!' Alex hissed.

'Here, take my hand, I'll pull you up this side and you can climb on that one!' Sarah urged her, ignoring her sister and excited by the challenge now.

Sarah half-pulled and Lily half-scrambled up between the two horses until she was able to get her leg over onto the other's back. The horse looked around, vaguely startled, but it didn't move as the girl got herself comfortable. Lily's face nearly split in two, she was smiling so much.

Sarah's mount swished her tail. Sarah thought for a moment the horse was about to bolt, but when she realised that it was not, she burst out laughing, startling both horses a bit.

'I thought she was off then!' Sarah exclaimed.

'Make them go,' Lily replied, kicking hers. The old horse was losing interest and lowered its head wearily. Sarah leant across and gave the horse a hard smack across the bottom.

The horse looked up, suddenly coming to life. Sarah whacked the horse again and it started to walk forward. Sarah whacked hers too and the second horse set off slowly after the first.

'Hey! That's mean!' Alex protested, but secretly she was envious.

Sarah reached up into an ash tree and snapped off a twig and then whacked Lily's mount from behind. Just then, a pheasant exploded from the grass at the horse's feet, startling the horse and with the sudden sting from the branch, it panicked and burst into an unexpectedly fast sprint for such an old animal. The sudden explosion of energy woke Sarah's horse up too and it was chasing after the other in the blink of an eye.

Both girls were startled and clung terrified to the horses' manes. Alex ran after them, terrified that they would be injured and it would be all her fault.

The terror the girls felt, exacerbated by their sense of guilt at behaving in a way that they knew would make their parents livid, was only multiplied when they suddenly heard a man's voice shouting at them.

'Hey! What are you doing?' The voice belonged to a figure holding a muck fork, an old woodsman. His face was horribly scarred from burns endured long ago. His right eye twisted down and the right side of his mouth pulled up into a vicious looking snarl. The whole of the right side of his head was, in fact, one nasty, old burn, while the hair on the left side of his head had been left to grow wild and untamed. His back was twisted and bent too, showing that the burns passed right down his right side, tightening the skin and restricting movement to such an extent that he limped and was stooping over.

Sarah screamed and threw herself from her horse. Lily

fell from hers at the same moment as she tried to dismount. Alex was petrified too. Helping the two younger girls up, she ran back towards the forest as fast as she could. Lily and Sarah rushed along behind her as fast as they could, rubbing their bruised limbs.

'Oh my God,' Sarah exclaimed. 'Did you see his face? It was actually melting!'

The horses ran back towards safety. The man watched the children bolt into the forest and slowly he lowered the muck fork. The blood drained from his face.

'No! Stay out of the forest!' he whispered shakily.

The girls ran deeper into the forest, as fast as they could. Looking back, Alex suddenly realised that she had left the other two a way behind. She stopped and peered into the dark shadows beneath the great fir trees. She couldn't see very far in any direction.

'Sarah?' she called. 'Lily? Where are you?'

She waited for a reply.

All she could hear was her own frantic breathing. Then there was a sound, a rustling sound of movement. She turned around sharply to see if she could see where that sound came from. Was it the wind in the trees? Again she heard the sound, but this time it came from another quarter and she spun round to focus on it.

'Hello? Sarah, Lily is that you?' she called out, silently cursing herself for having lost the younger girls again.

There it was again – the sound – behind her again; she turned again. But there was nothing there but shadows and trees.

'Where are you both?' she cried out desperately.

Snap!

Behind her somewhere, a twig snapped.

'SARAH!' she called. 'SARAH! LILY!'

She paused to listen for a reply.

Suddenly, she heard a girl's scream, far off across the wood. Without hesitating, she ran off into the trees towards the place the cry had come from. She was crashing through the dense forest now; the lower limbs of the fir trees were dead and hard as they scratched at her face and arms as she pushed through. 'SARAH! LILY! WHERE ARE YOU?'

A voice called out to her; it was too far away to make out who it was from, but Alex changed direction to head to where the sound had come from. 'SARAH, LILY!'

'We're here!' came back the distant, plaintive cry from Sarah. Alex headed down through the trees towards the sound. 'Alex! We're over here...'

Alex pushed on, the vicious, brittle branches ripping at her face. 'I'm coming, where are you?'

'We're here!' Lily called out as she saw Alex coming through the dense trees.

'Are you okay?' Alex asked anxiously as she ran up to the two younger girls. 'I heard a scream!'

'It was me; something was following us. I thought it was still the man with the burnt face chasing us, but it wasn't' Lily responded, throwing her arms around Alex.

'Are you sure it wasn't him?' Alex said looking into the forest, expecting the woodsman to appear at any moment. 'There are so many trees, it'd be hard to see who it was.'

'No, it definitely wasn't an old man,' Sarah said, her face ashen. Alex turned to Sarah and the look of her made Alex's blood run cold.

'It might have been an alien,' Sarah said quietly.

'Or a goblin,' Lily added, equally softly.

Alex sighed and smiled. Relieved now because she knew it could be neither. 'Okay, come on, let's go.'

'Don't you believe us?' Lily asked quietly. Sarah just turned angrily away.

Reluctantly, both girls got up to their feet and followed Alex, neither wanted to be left behind.

'This is silly,' Alex said, trying to calm them both down. 'It was probably just an animal or some...'

'It wasn't!' Sarah snapped back angrily.

'Well maybe you're wrong and it was the burnt old man, maybe he's looking for us, maybe he's still cross about his horses,' Alex replied.

'Are you calling me a liar?' Sarah demanded.

'No, of course not,' Alex said. 'Sometimes, when we're scared and in this light...'

'I saw what I saw!' Sarah snapped.

'What was it then?' Lily asked quietly. They all stopped and waited for Sarah to speak. Sarah looked around for movement before she spoke.

'I don't know,' Sarah muttered. 'It looked human, but it wasn't.'

They waited for her to say something else, but she didn't. ...

Instead, they heard the noise of sudden movement in the forest.

'There's something up there!' Sarah shrieked and she began to cry.

'RUN!' Alex screamed. All three fled through the forest.

Behind them, they could hear something rushing towards them.

The ground in this part of the forest was fairly flat, but the trees were densely packed, with thick growths of alder, willow and birch. Running through them was like an assault course from hell. The undergrowth was thick too, and the girls were soon crashing through fallen branches and trees and thick bramble. And behind them, whatever was following was crashing through the undergrowth too.

They could hear heavy running feet, snapping branches and heavy breathing.

Suddenly, they crashed out onto a narrow path. It led steeply downwards, or upwards into what looked like an overgrown mass of briars.

'Which way?' Lily asked.

'That way,' she urged, pointing down the hill.

'That's TOO STEEP TO GET DOWN' Sarah screamed.

'Just GO!' Alex barked, turning to face the rapidly approaching creature, thrashing through the undergrowth behind them. Alex took a deep breath and grabbed the thickest stick she could find to wield like a club. 'I've got this!'

Suddenly a wild animal crashed through the undergrowth, screaming in rage. It was all teeth and long hair and mud. Two tiny black eyes raged at them. And giant fangs! Two giant, white fangs!

It charged straight away, hurtling towards the horror-struck Alex.

Alex prepared to die. The beast smashed into her knocking her to the ground and winding her, then tossed her aside like a rag doll. She grabbed a branch from the litter and beat at the beast's snarling teeth.

Something whooshed past Alex's head and with a sickening crunch, thumped into the beast's head.

It was an axe.

The beast dropped dead at Alex's feet, the axe embedded in its skull. She whipped around to see where the axe had come from. It was the old woodsman. He looked even more savage and angry. Lily screamed and she and

Sarah ran off. Alex scrambled to her feet, wide eyed and ran after the others.

He's saved me she thought as she ran, but she was still too terrified of the burnt old man to do anything other than run from him as fast as she could.

'NO!' shouted the woodsman, but to no avail; the girls were in full flight, running as fast as they could from him and he knew that he wouldn't be able to catch them. With a deep sigh, he retrieved his axe from the skull of the giant wild boar and dragging his right leg, nevertheless staggered after them.

The girls raced down a steep, densely forested ravine. Fallen trees and broken limbs blocked them at every turn. Their hair snagged on branches. Sharp twigs ripped their clothes and any exposed skin. It felt like a thousand bony fingers snatching at them in their blind panic. Suddenly, Alex lost her footing and fell down the steep bank, sliding in the mud and a carpet of mossy pine needles, down under fallen branches and lodged trees. She desperately grabbed at a branch to stop herself falling further, but it was no use; the branch was rotten and snapped and she fell down the hill at painful speed, twisting her ankle as she landed at the bottom.

Lily and Sarah's descent was steadier and less seriously injurious, but still painful. Sarah was rubbing a skinned knee and picking bits of leaf and detritus from the forest floor out of the graze.

'I just want to go home!' Lily wailed.

High above them, they could still hear the sound of movement.

'It's the old man. He's still after us,' Sarah said. 'We've got to keep moving.'

Alex was going to find that difficult. 'Help me up,' she said. 'Pass me that stick.'

Sarah picked up the large, thick branch Alex had indicated and passed it to her.

Alex tried to stand, only to find the pain excruciating when she put her weight on her injured ankle. She sat back down and undressed her foot, removing the lace-up boot and carefully unrolling the sock.

The ankle was inflated to an extraordinary size and was already starting to turn from red to purple.

'Ohh!' Lily said, stepping back from it.

'Yuk, nasty!' Sarah added helpfully.

For a moment, they all just sat and stared at the foot, not knowing quite what to do. Not far from them was a river.

'Help me up,' Alex said finally. 'It's red hot; perhaps if I let it soak in the river it will cool down and be less painful. It might even stop it swelling up any more,'

Alex made her way, carefully, to the river bank with Lily and Sarah's help. There she sat down on a large boulder and dangled her sore foot in the brook.

The comfort it provided was both short-lived and did little to ease the swelling. The party of three were all tired, hungry, and afraid at being lost in the woods, not to mention their fear of the burnt old man. The sky was darkening and they decided they must keep moving.

Alex struggled to put her boot back on. The other two came over and tried to help, but her ankle had swollen far too much. Every time they tried to get the boot on, it caused too much pain for Alex. They tried pulling out the laces altogether and forcing the tongue and flaps out as wide as they could, but still the boot would not go on.

'Stop it, it hurts!' Alex protested.

'What're we goin' to do?' Lily asked. 'How're we going to get out of here if you can't walk?'

Alex took her T-shirt off and knotted it around her leg and foot. She reached for the long branch and began to pull herself up with it. It hurt like crazy and she grimaced in pain. To make things worse, the going was going to be very difficult now they were at the bottom of a steep gully strewn with boulders.

'Come on,' Alex said to the others, 'we'll have to go up the river. There must be a road or something that crosses it up there, back to the castle.'

'How d'you know?' Sarah snarled.

'I don't,' Alex replied. 'But that doesn't mean there isn't one!'

Just then, it began to rain and rain very hard. Within moments the girls were wet through.

'Come on,' Alex said softly to Sarah, touching her arm reassuringly. Sarah pulled her arm away.

Lily moved forward and took Alex's arm. Alex smiled gratefully at the younger girl. Sarah moved forward and, in a change of heart, took her sister's other arm – after all, they were all in this together. Alex smiled at her younger sister, and the latter smiled back weakly.

'Thanks,' Alex said quietly, rain running down her face.

'Let's go,' Sarah replied. 'We're getting wet. At least under that tree, we might find a dry spot.'

They hobbled over the rocks to the yew tree. There, pressed hard against the gnarly old trunk, they were, at least, out of the worst of the rain. Even so, every now and then, big fat raindrops would drip from the higher branches and fall on the soaked children with a heavy plop.

'This is no good,' Alex said, looking at the shivering girls next to her. 'We need to find shelter…shit, what's that?'

In a fork in the tree was an animal's skull. It looked as though it had been placed there deliberately. With a shiver, Alex grabbed the creepy skull and tossed it into the river as far away as she could.

Through the sound of the rain, they heard sounds in the forest that unsettled them too, even more than the skull had done.

'What is that?' Lily whispered.

'I don't know, I thought I heard...' Alex paused as she peered into the thickening weather. 'Voices. Distant voices. Perhaps someone's coming.'

'Maybe they're looking for us,' Lily suggested half-heartedly, doubting her own words as she uttered them, and certainly not about to call out to the voices for help.

'No,' Alex replied slowly. 'It's kind of an angry whispering.'

The rain continued to fall heavily. White frothy trails of water were running down the Yew tree's trunk and were collecting into little foamy patches at the tree's roots. The previously clear water of the river had been replaced by a roaring muddy brown torrent. The girls were hugging each other, partly to hold Alex up, partly for warmth and partly for security.

Lightning intermittently filled the darkening valley with blinding light, and thunder crashed about them. The girls were petrified. The valley seemed full of strange dark shapes as the boulders were lit from behind. Alex wondered if she saw one of the rocks move in that brief flash.

'Come on,' Alex urged them, 'we can't stay here under this tree; lightning always hits the tallest tree.'

Carefully, the girls began to pick their way upstream again, through the torrential rain, their wet clothes clinging to their skin. Their hair fell in bedraggled and soaking tendrils down their faces.

The further the girls moved forward, the craggier the sides of the valley grew. The going was slow with Alex complaining to the younger girls that she couldn't move any faster.

'Let me rest for a minute,' she pleaded. 'We can hide behind one of the big rocks.'

As they approached the biggest rock, they saw a tree had fallen down the bank and was lodged against the foot of the cliff.

'There, behind that tree root!' Alex pointed. They all climbed up the side of the fallen tree and there they found a cave at the foot of the cliff, hidden behind the fallen oak tree. A small, dark cave, but nevertheless out of the rain.

They needed no second look, and carefully they made their way behind the endless columns of running water dribbling down the cliff face. It was cold and clammy in the muddy cave, but it offered some shelter.

Alex sat down at the cave mouth, just inside of the streams of running water, and Sarah and Lily huddled together just beyond her, trying to get warm.

'We need a fire,' Alex observed.

They were all silent for a moment, thinking. Lily started to rock back and forth.

'What's up?' Alex asked.

'Tummy ache,' Lily replied.

'Cramps?' Alex asked suddenly. Lily nodded. 'Are you having your period?'

Lily blushed. 'Don't know, never had one.'

Alex stared, wide-eyed at Lily. 'Your first?'

'Yes, why?' Lily had heard the concern in Alex's voice. Alex jumped up and despite the pain in her leg she went to the cave entrance and stared out. 'What? What is it?'

Alex gazed out of the cave mouth biting her lip.

The scene was lit suddenly with lightning and a few moments later thunder rolled threateningly through the valley. She said nothing for a moment. 'It looks like the storm is passing anyway,'

'So who's whispering about us?' Lily said. Alex shivered again.

'I don't know, Lily,' Alex replied. 'Maybe it's just a trick of the wind, blowing through the leaves on the trees. Maybe there's someone out there trying to frighten us. I don't know. But I do know that the best way for us to get out of here is to follow the river.'

'When the rain stops,' Sarah urged. 'Maybe they're still out there.'

'I don't know that we can wait,' Alex replied. 'It seems to be getting darker all the time; we don't want to spend the night here, do we?'

'I'd rather be in this cave than out there!' Lily declared.

'Yes, it wouldn't be so bad, if we had a fire,' Sarah agreed.

'Maybe, we could rub some sticks together and make a fire!' Lily suggested.

'Where are we going to get some dry sticks from?' Sarah asked. 'Everything out there is wet through!'

'When the lightening flashed, I thought I saw some sticks here.' She fumbled around in the darkness. 'Yes, no wait, they're sort of tied together or something.'

Lily held the sticks up in the faint light from the cave entrance, trying to make it out. Just then a flash of light from the disappearing storm lit up the cave faintly and they all saw the shape of the sticks illuminated. The sticks were tied in the shape of a pentangle in a circle.

Lily dropped it quickly.

'What's that?' Sarah asked.

'Witchcraft!' Alex replied, grabbing it and breaking it up. 'Children playing, perhaps, I don't know. Look the rain is letting off a bit; maybe we could get going in a minute.'

The other two didn't look that keen at the prospect of going back into the rain, so for a while they all just sat there and waited. The rain did seem less now, but it still fell relentlessly down beyond the cave. The river continued to get deeper and louder. The mist and spume filled the air, so even though they weren't getting rained on, they weren't going to get any dryer either.

Just then, a large bat, confused by the darkness outside, flew out of a crevice in the back of the cave. On seeing the bat, Lily screamed, and within seconds all three were back out into the rain again.

Mist rolled across the valley floor after the rain, as the girls picked their way through the boulders and rocks covered in thick, green moss. Every step was a painful experience for Alex as she made her way along using the branch as a makeshift crutch.

'Maybe it's ghosts,' Sarah offered, as she followed Alex.

Alex stopped and looked witheringly at her sister. 'Really?' she replied. Then, she turned away again and continued to pick her way through the rocks.

'Well, you don't know everything,' Sarah offered grumpily in response.

'Just shut up will you!' Alex snapped back. 'I just want to get out of this bloody forest, okay? It's not ghosts, it's not monsters or aliens, it's just wind in the trees! Now shut up and help me.'

Petulantly, Sarah took Alex's arm and helped her climb over a particularly large boulder at the foot of the cliff overhanging the river. Just then, a small trail of rocks came crashing down the cliff from above. The girls crouched down, protecting their heads in case rocks hit them, but as fast as the rock fall had begun, it now ceased. Alex looked urgently about them to check that the other two were not hurt, and then she looked up the cliff to see where the tiny avalanche had come from.

'What was that?' Lily asked, peering up into the forest above.

'Nothing,' Alex replied, without conviction.

'There's someone or something up there,' Sarah said fearfully.

The three girls anxiously looked this way and that as they tried to identify the source of the rockfall.

'It's nothing,' Alex said, grasping her fallen stick and the big rock and trying to pull herself over it. 'All this rain probably just washed out a rock, that's all.'

Sarah moved to help Alex, but Lily was still looking upward.

'Come on Lily!' Alex urged. Lily looked around and realised that the other two had gone over the big rock and were moving on. She hurried to follow.

A fresh trail of small pebbles and dirt slipped down the cliff face behind her. She whirled around, but there was nothing there. She hurried to catch the others up, then suddenly looked up the cliff face. High above, the light caught two eyes and a shape moved quickly out of sight. She screamed.

'What is it?' Alex called, spinning around. Sarah came scrambling down the steep river bank next to her.

Lily looked around and as she did, she thought she could hear strange whispering coming up out from the woods on all sides. Voices, tiny voices. The wind in the grass or leaves dancing. But more urgent, more sinister, more dangerous. And it was coming towards them. The blood drained from her face.

'What's that?' Sarah asked.

'Run,' Alex said quietly. But no one moved, their legs turned to stone as they looked around them. Shapes moved through the shadows. Vaguely human and yet bent and twisted over.

'RUN!' Alex screamed, pushing the girls up the forest track. The girls suddenly came to life and set off again with all the strength and speed that they could muster. The pain in her ankle held Alex up, but the sight behind her pushed her forward, and she ran after the others with all her strength.

They ran until their lungs were on fire. Lily and Sarah left Alex behind, but she valiantly tried to catch them. As they ran, they saw lights appearing in the darkness of the forest. Voices mocked them from the shadows.

'We're being herded,' Alex whispered as she ran, looking about her at the strange lights all around, but there was nothing else she could make out, only shapes.

'Lily!' a woman's voice called out in the distance.

'Mum?' Lily shrieked, turning towards the voice.

'Lily!' her name came floating back from the hill. The girls all ran towards the voice with renewed vigour, up through dense conifers ripping at their faces and snatching at their clothes, relieved that their nightmare promised to be at an end.

Suddenly they emerged from the blackness of the forest into what seemed like a clearing, deep in shadow.

'Lily,' Mallory White called gently.

'Mum!' Lily ran towards the voice, seeing in the middle of the clearing the dark outline of her mother with another figure standing close to her. They both appeared to be dressed in robes.

Alex ran out of the wood and slowed to a stumble. 'No,' she whispered. 'Something's not right here. No, Lily!'

But it was too late. Lily was in the arms of her mother in the middle of the clearing. All around the outside, along the forest edges, in every direction, lights were emerging from the shadows.

Alex slowed to a walk, turning to look for a way to retreat. She found that there were lights emerging from behind her too. They were completely surrounded. Boxed in. Trapped.

'Hello Lily White,' Lord Morgan said.

Lily looked up suddenly in fright at her mother. Her mother just smiled back a cold, heartless smile.

'Welcome to forest on this midsummer's night,' Morgan continued. 'This is a very important moment for us, do you know why?'

Lily shook her head slowly, a sense of foreboding growing inside her.

'Your mother tells me that you are menstruating for the first time? Is this true?' Morgan asked. Lily felt ashamed, and lowered her head, nodding slowly. Morgan took her chin and lifted it; smiling, he looked down at her. 'There is nothing to be ashamed of child. This is a powerful, magical moment in your life. And you had to come here because of it. It was important that you came into the forest. And it was important that you came of your own volition. That's why we both told you not to go into the forest, because we knew you would disobey. A menarche here on midsummer's eve, my dear friends here have waited a long time for this.'

Out of the shadows figures had emerged, and now they

were standing in a circle, holding burning wooden torches aloft.

'Let her go,' Alex said in voice that came out sounding weaker than she'd wanted it. Shaking, she stepped forward, fists clenched.

Morgan laughed. 'Seize her. Light the fires.'

Alex was grabbed from behind before she could move. Fire leapt up in a circle around the ring of stones, casting long shadows.

'Let us begin,' Lord Morgan said.

Mallory, still holding Lily's hand dragged her reluctant daughter towards a large flat stone, covered in a red velvet cloth embroidered with a golden pentacle. Around the altar, lit by the dancing flames, was a ring of twelve standing stones. Beyond the circle of stone lay the darkness of the forest, shrouding the clearing form the outside world.

Beyond the burning fire, on the edge of the forest, his face lit by dancing flames, stood the old woodsman holding his axe.

'Not again,' he muttered to himself. Tightening the grip on his axe, he leapt into the circle of fire.

THE ANGEL'S KISS

S.J. Menary

I heard him over the bar. He didn't know I was listening.

'Listen up, you'll never believe this!' he said in a gruff whisper. 'You'll never in a thousand years guess what I'm about to tell you, Bill mate!' He grabbed Bill's sleeve.

'Well? Spit it out then,' Bill wrenched his arm away. Bill was a regular. A big bloke, every night I'd see him slouched against the bar squinting into his beard and picking out flecks of dried blood.

'I saw her!' said the other one, waving his hands. He was nothing like Bill. Short and skinny, fragile looking, like he might snap in two if the wind blew too hard.

'Who?' said Bill.

'The angel,' the skinny one replied.

'You what?'

'The angel! The one everyone's been talking about! Dear God man, have you got wax in your ears?'

'I dunno what you're on about, Ed,' Bill took a chug of his drink.

Ed huffed, leaning heavily onto my bar. His fingers smeared the residual grease across the wood. I forced myself not to push him off and start polishing right then and there. Instead, I poured a slow pint of beer and let the froth settle. Nudging closer, I strained to hear the rest of their conversation.

153

'Alright then, Bill,' Ed snorted. 'You're too stupid to know what's going on anyhow.'

'I am not stupid!' Bill slammed his tankard down onto the bar, making both Ed and me jump. 'I just been out of town for a bit, s'all.'

'Bill, I didn't mean anything by it, you know that right, mate?'

Bill gave Ed a long stare, and then shrugged his shoulders. 'A'right. Tell us about this gal then.'

'Everyone's been talking about it. Old Sal's lad saw her first. There, in the wheat field just before dawn. Damn fainted at the shock, he did! But then, he was always a soppy one, Old Sal's lad. No one paid it much mind, though. Not until Dunstable done saw 'er too! Ain't no one gonna argue the toss with a vicar, now, are they? He said he saw her at the lake. "A Vision from the Lord God Almighty" 'e said.'

'Huh?'

'Yep.'

'Uh.'

'And Larry the baker. He saw her too. And Larry's wife, 'er mother, their six kids. Saw her at the fair, they did,' Ed blabbered.

'So when did you see 'er?' Bill took another swig.

'It were that frosty morning the other day. There she were, bold as brass! Standing by the well, all surrounded by mist and that. Just a girl. Young, like. Pretty. She had this, dark black hair all flowing and really pale skin.'

'She have big…?'

'Shurrup! I was visited by an angel from God, you idiot!'

Bill stifled a laugh, blowing froth off his beer and covering his beard with creamy bubbles. 'Sorry, Ed. Carry on, mate.'

'She were wearing this dress-thing, all made out of golden feathers, just floatin' around her. Wings like an angel, gold and glittery. I ain't seen nuffin like it, Bill, I'm tellin' ya!'

'Pah! Bollocks! It was just some lass, you dolt!'

'No way! It were an angel!'

'It were last night's mead.'

'I swear it!'

'Your imagination's playin' tricks. Bad meat. Fever. Delusions! A ghost?'

'Bill, she were real! She weren't no apparition!'

'And what would an angel sent by the Almighty 'imself be doin' in our town, huh? Why would a divine angel o' the Lord present 'erself to Ed the local drunkard?' Bill scoffed.

'How the 'ell would I know? Cleanse me o' my sins? Show me God's true path?' Ed spat.

'You're talkin' outta your arse, man,' Bill chuckled.

'Yeah? Well, I'll show you who's talkin' out o' their arse!'

Ed hurled a punch, missed, and cracked against my bar. There was a howl of pain. Bill heaved as he lifted Ed up into the air, hurling him bodily across the bar. He crashed in a heap of tables, customers and flagons. There was a collective roar from the tavern's customers, and in one breath the bar erupted into chaos. Ale hurtled across the room, chairs snapped as they were broken across people's backs, punches swinging left and right.

I ducked below the bar as a bottle flew towards me, smashing in a cascade of liquor and shattered green glass. Time to make a sharp exit, I thought, and scurried away in a rather undignified arse-in-the-air crawling run.

Looking back at the uproar in the tavern, I flinched as the silhouetted figures upturned the tables. I could hear the landlord yelling at the top of his lungs. Damn it all, but that was going to be my job to clear up in the morning.

For now, I just breathed in the crisp night air. Ed and Bill, what a pair of idiots. But then again, what they had said had got me thinking. That story about the angel girl. I wandered out into the dark streets, past the well where Ed said he'd seen her.

What if it was true? The mists were slinking in again, and my shoes were wet from the moist air. What if there was an angel, here, in this town? To show us the true path to goodness?

I walked a little further, until I reached the square. And then I stopped.

Breath caught.

Blood turned to ice.

She was there. Standing on the far side of the square, shrouded in grey fog. Her hair fell long and dark like shimmering midnight. But that dress. It glowed like the sunset; bright, burnished gold. Long, delicate feathers caressed her pale skin.

And those eyes. Black as the sky above. Piercing. Staring right at me.

I was entranced, transfixed. Paralysed with the most overwhelming rush of awe and fear and love. It was like nothing I had known before. Total intoxication.

She moved silently, floating towards me until I could almost reach out. Touch that alabaster skin, those soft feathers, those eyes... She moved nearer, until I was breathing the very same air as her.

In those few seconds, I was hers. Complete, perfectly, and without hesitation.

She pulled me to her, reaching for me with her exquisite lips. Inching closer, closer, closer. Until, with agonising ecstasy, she kissed me.

* * *

'Oh, Bill, mate, I am so hungover!'

'Don't Ed. Just don't.'

They staggered through the square, blinking in the harsh, burning light of unforgiving morning.

'What did we drink last night??'

'Mead, ale, beer, cider...' Bill growled.

'Uh, I'm gonna throw up...' Ed clutched his stomach.

'Fry-up?' Bill whacked Ed forcefully on the back, a smile creasing under his beard as his friend turned a pale shade of green.

'They keep a special place in Hell for people like you, Bill.'

'C'mon, you'll feel better.'

'You know, it'll all come back upppparrgh!'

Bill looked back to see Ed, crumpled on the floor where he had tripped. 'Look, we don't have to eat, man.' Bill looked at his feet apologetically.

Ed clawed his way back up, a confused look on his face. They both peered down to see what he had tripped over.

'Bloody Hell,' Ed cursed.

Staring up at them from the cobble stones were the glassy eyes of a dead boy. In the bartender's hand, he clutched a single golden feather.

TOLD YOU SO

Mark A. Smart

I. Hopley

The world was silent. Silent except for the wailing siren.

It's a test. It has to be.

Stuart Hopley looked around the supermarket. Everyone had stopped what they were doing, confused. Some with products in hand, hovering above a trolley.

The silence was suddenly broken by a cacophony of sound as every mobile phone in the store woke up at once to alert their faithful slaves of a new incoming message. Hopley gazed at the notification: *UK Government Emergency Messaging Service: Air Attack Warning. Find cover at once.*

People dropped whatever they were carrying. The beeping of phones replaced by the screams of scared, panicking shoppers.

Don't panic, Stuart. You need food and water. Tins, cans, processed food. Vitamins and painkillers.

He heard glass smash as people threw baskets and trolleys through the plate glass windows at the front of the store in their rush to leave, the main entrance already a crush of people.

He probably had less than a minute left to find a place to protect himself from the blast. He glanced around and noticed he was stood next to a chest freezer. He slid back the transparent lid, removed some pies, climbed in and rolled into a foetal position. He closed his eyes and covered his ears with his hands.

Just over a mile above the centre of Leicester, a nuclear warhead detonated. A millisecond of brilliant white light preceded a raging fireball which expanded from the blast-point destroying everything within a half-mile radius. Super-heated air set fire to everything in its path; anybody caught in the open was vaporised.

As the fireball expanded upward and outward, a shock wave started its destructive journey, reaching speeds of around four hundred miles per hour. It tore across Leicester, making buildings explode due to the change in air pressure it created. As it moved outwards from the epicentre, its power slowly diminished, and when it hit the Tesco Superstore in the southern suburb of Wigston it was travelling at around one-hundred and eighty miles an hour, catching up with the heatwave which was still hot enough to cause third-degree burns on exposed skin.

Hopley felt the building rock. The noise was deafening. He opened his eyes to see that the roof of the store had been torn off. The sky grey and full of debris. But then, less than a minute after the explosion, calm returned. Hopley saw a blue sky through a gap in the dust and for a moment everything seemed strangely normal, apart from being sat in a freezer.

I need better cover, he thought as he reached for the lid of the freezer. Tentatively, he slid it back and stood. He hadn't really taken in until now how the temperature inside the freezer had changed from freezing cold to unpleasantly hot as the heatwave had melted and then started to boil the ice in the freezer.

He climbed out the freezer and looked around, spotting the entrance to what he assumed was the stockroom at the back of the store. Ignoring the moans of the injured and dying, he picked up his trolley, which had been blown over in the blast, scattering its load. He quickly refilled it, and ran with it through the wide entrance he had seen, finding himself in a small warehouse.

He could see the loading bay doors open along one side of the warehouse. The warehouse staff had abandoned their forklifts and pallet trolleys. There was no one about.

He needed somewhere safe, safe from fallout, the invisible killer. The cold room was the obvious place. It was self-contained and stored food. The perfect solution.

Hopley made his way to the cold room. It was dark, it was cold, it was home for now. The room had its own loading bay, the door having a translucent perspex window that was somehow still intact. Hopley went in and closed the door.

II. Dean

Michael Dean curled up in the corner of the cellar of what used to be The 1852 public house, located on Station Road in Wigston. He'd bought the pub just a month earlier, hoping to convert it into flats.

The second global financial crisis of the twenty-first century had struck in 2020 and had been good news for Dean, as there were plenty of properties to buy and let to those who couldn't afford a mortgage. This old pub was to be converted into three apartments. Aged fifty-two, Dean had been looking forward to retiring very soon, having amassed a fortune by preying on those who had fallen on hard times.

An unscrupulous businessman, Dean would use anybody for self-gain, as long as they weren't confrontational. He portrayed the kind of self-confidence that very few would go against, but it was just a front. Anyone who knew him well would know that he'd back down at the slightest protest to anything he suggested. But his build and persona kept people at arm's length and kept Dean on the winning side of most negotiations.

As civilisation fell around him, he lay on the cold cellar floor and wondered how things could have gone so devastatingly wrong.

His gloomy thought was interrupted by calm. The sirens had stopped a few minutes ago, just before the lights went out and the building started shaking. The winds had now abated. Was it over? Was the worst of it over or was the worst still to come?

He stood up, but couldn't see anything as the cellar was in darkness. He took his phone from his pocket, switched on the torch, looking for the flashlight he always took with him when he was working beneath ground level. He saw beer barrels, cases of spirits, mixers and soft drinks, boxes of crisps and nuts and other snacks; but was there enough to live on until the all-clear sounded? Dean shone the beam of light around the cellar once more. *Shit. Where am I supposed to... shit?*

For the next two weeks both Hopley and Dean survived on their meagre supplies, each one not knowing the other existed, even though they were only separated by a disused drum factory and a railway line.

Neither showed signs of radiation sickness. Neither was bothered by other survivors scavenging for food or water. Both, on several occasions, thought about taking their own life. Neither did. That hard-coded instruction in human programming coming to the fore: survive at any cost.

It was lack of food and drinking water that forced Dean's hand. He'd spent two weeks living on crisps, nuts and booze, and he was feeling the adverse effects of such a poor diet. He was still alive, granted, but his food was running out and he couldn't stand the thought of surviving a nuclear war just to die of liver failure. He made the decision to leave the cellar, despite the fact that the all-clear hadn't yet sounded. He doubted it ever would.

He moved the heavy beer barrels he'd used to barricade the entrance and slowly opened the door. He wasn't sure what he'd be facing when he opened the door at the top of the stairs. He made a slow ascent up the dark staircase.

Reaching the door at the top of the stairs he stopped. Taking a deep breath, he reached for the door handle. He pressed his ear to the door to see if he could hear anything on the other side. He'd give anything to hear people playing pool, watching football on TV, enjoying a normal life.

Exhaling, he twisted the handle. The door opened with a moan. He looked through the narrow gap and the first thing that hit his mind was grey. Everything was coated in dust, ash and soot. The room was empty, as he knew it would be. As he tried to open the door further, it got caught on an obstacle and wouldn't move. He pushed a little harder and the obstruction gave a little. He stopped when he heard a scratching sound, then saw a rat run across the room. Its snout looked dark and wet, its eyes menacing. It stopped for a moment and seemed to size up Dean. Dean could almost read its mind: *It's a live one. Is it worth the risk?* Apparently, he wasn't, as the rat turned and scurried off.

Dean tried the door again. He could get his head and shoulders through it, but it was still stuck on something. He stretched as much as he could, to try and see what was behind the door and instantly wished he hadn't. A body lay on the dust-covered floor. Somebody who'd survived the blast, and then sought refuge in the pub.

Where the body wasn't burnt it had been eaten. And judging by the amount of blood, Dean surmised that it had been quite a recent demise. The poor soul had been suffering a long and painful death from radiation sickness before the rat came calling for lunch. Dean struggled to keep down what little contents his stomach contained.

I have to get out of here, he thought. *I have to find food. Tesco.*

III. A raw meet

Come on, Stu-boy. It's time.

Hopley pushed open the cold room door and, to his amazement, nothing had really changed since he'd gone in two weeks ago. But then, it wouldn't have. The blast had already happened when he'd gone into the cold room. Little was going to change, except for the dust.

He noticed the same grey as Dean had, like the world had run out of coloured ink and nobody could afford a new toner cartridge. The warehouse building was still intact, just. The walls, unlike the main store, were brick and though there was some minor damage to the roof, the structure seemed intact and it didn't look like anybody had been snooping around.

First job, sanitation. He had to remove the dead from the store. He decided to leave them outside in the yard beyond the loading bays. There's no reason anybody would go there: there was no point. He'd be sure to close the gates at some point too, just to protect himself a bit more.

The second job, make the place as uninviting to looters and scavengers as was possible. This meant moving some corpses to the front of the store. He had to be careful not to make it too obvious that somebody was inside, but make it as uninviting as possible, like the reward wasn't worth the effort. This also meant stripping the shelves of just about everything, whether he could use it or not, and making the task of moving through the store as inconvenient as possible.

Third job. That would have to wait.

What's that noise?

Hopley peered through the warehouse door into the devastated store beyond. His gaze was instantly drawn to a man trying to make his way through the ruins of the supermarket.

He was a big man, intimidating; but he looked lost, not in a didn't-know-where-he-was way, but emotionally and mentally lost. No surprise really, given all that had happened.

Suddenly there was a crash from the front of the store. The man didn't seem to notice, but Hopley could hear the faint sounds of a number of voices and doubted their intentions were noble.

The big man was still aimlessly wandering toward Hopley, climbing over fallen shelves and manoeuvring through the remains of capitalism.

Hopley stepped into the store and waved his arms, trying to get the other's attention. Eventually, the other man looked up and noticed Hopley.

Come here, quick, Hopley mouthed.

The big man suddenly got the message and started a short but perilous trip toward Hopley. A smile formed on the big man's face as he approached. A smile that quickly turned into a menacing grimace as he pulled a knife from the waistband at the back of his jeans. He swung the blade wildly at Hopley, who managed to step back out of the way, shocked by the sudden change of events. But no sooner had it started than it was over. A loud metallic thump was followed by the knife-wielding man falling to the floor. Hopley looked up to see another man stood holding a fire extinguisher. That man was Dean.

'Come on,' said Hopley to the stranger who had come to his rescue, 'we need to get out of here.'

Hopley hurried Dean into the warehouse moments before a group of men turned onto the far end of the aisle directly opposite the warehouse entrance.

The two men ran as best they could through the debris and detritus in the warehouse. Not to the cold room, but to the open loading bay doors where they jumped down into the loading yard beyond.

'Where are we going?' Dean asked, a little out of breath.

'Just getting some cover until they leave,' replied Hopley. 'There's a lot of stuff in there I could use.'

'You could use?' Dean asked. 'You wouldn't have had the chance if I hadn't just saved you.'

Hopley stopped and turned to Dean. 'And now I'm saving you, so I'd say we're even. Now let's get the hell out of here before we're both killed.'

'Follow me,' instructed Dean as he headed to the open gate to the yard. Turning right once through the gates, they jumped a low wooden fence and headed into a row of trees. 'The railway line is just over there,' said Dean, 'past the old drum factory.' Hopley looked at the building as Dean continued explaining his plan. 'I've been hiding in a pub, just the other side of the tracks. We could wait there and go back to Tesco later.'

'Lead the way,' said Hopley.

IV. Time, gentlemen, please

A few minutes later, the two men were crossing the railway lines, taking care to make sure nothing was coming before crossing, though they both knew no trains would be making the trip to London for a very long time, if ever at all.

'Not from these parts, then?' Dean asked.

'What? How do you know that?' Hopley countered.

'The football shirt,' said Dean pointing at Hopley's dirty attire.

'I don't think there are too many Southampton fans in Leicester. We have our own sub-par team to support. Though I once knew a Cheltenham Town fan who lived here, wonder what he's up to these days?'

Hopley laughed. He couldn't help himself. 'Well, he's probably dead. Have you spent the last couple of weeks sleeping? I'm from Romsey. Hampshire. Not far from Southampton. I'm working,' he paused, looking around with a furrowed brow, 'was working up here. Construction.' They were on Station Road. A quaint row of terraced cottages was somehow still standing.

'Funny,' said Dean. 'The damage doesn't look too bad from here.'

Hopley surveyed the row of cottages. 'That last house would've taken the majority of the blast when it got here, shielding the rest of the row. Assuming the city centre was hit, of course.'

He turned back to Dean and held a hand out gesturing for the other man to lead the way. Dean turned and started walking toward the pub. Hopley fell in line beside him.

'We were lucky,' Hopley continued.

'Lucky?!' Dean asked incredulously. 'World war bloody three breaks out and we're lucky?'

'It was a small bomb. Not a megaton device, that's for sure.'

'What makes you say that?'

'We wouldn't be here if it was.'

Dean started to reply but was cut short.

'Shhh,' Hopley said as he tilted his head to the left.

Dean's gaze followed to see a dog, Labrador-sized but neither could say what breed it was, that had just wandered out of an alleyway. It was a skinny, shabby looking thing. Its ribcage was showing and it had matted, tangled fur. It looked hungry, sniffing the ground hoping for a scent that would lead it to food. It was joined by a second, smaller dog that had a glint of mad ferocity in its eye.

The two men took an involuntary step back, the movement alerting the dogs to their presence. The smaller dog bared its teeth and growled, hackles raising down its back. It took a step forward, never taking its eyes off Hopley who bent down and picked up a stone from the side of the road. The pub door was mere yards away; the dogs stood between the men and the entrance.

'When I say run,' Hopley ordered, 'run, just sprint for the door.'

Hopley suddenly took a leap forward, shouting loudly in a rage and swinging his arms in the air.

The dogs, startled by this action, cowered for a moment and took a couple of steps back into the alley.

'Run!' Hopley shouted. He threw the stone at the smaller of the two dogs, hoping it was the alpha, hitting the dog on the head. It let out a whimper.

Dean was through the doorway, into the pub. Hopley followed and pushed the door behind him, but it didn't shut properly. The thud of a dog running into it followed, and it swung open, creaking on its hinges. Dean ran toward the cellar door. The corpse, which was now nearly unrecognisable as something which was once a living, breathing human, was now feeding four or five rats, which hissed at Dean as he opened the door leading to the stairway, to safety.

The dogs were in pursuit but struggled to gain purchase on the wooden floor. As Hopley grabbed the door frame and propelled himself down the stairs, the dogs slid by, into the corpse, into the rats.

Hopley slammed the door shut and headed into the total darkness below. He got to the bottom and was suddenly blinded as Dean turned on the flashlight directly into his eyes.

'What the fuck!' Hopley swung his arm knocking the torch away.

'Sorry,' replied a sheepish Dean. 'Close the bottom door, will you?'

Hopley closed the door and leant back against it, letting out a long breath. 'Jesus, that was close,' he said, followed by, 'I'm Stuart, Stuart Hopley. Appreciate what you did in the shop.' The beam of light was still shining in his direction, but not directly in his eyes, casting Dean in silhouette.

'Michael Dean.'

'Well, Mike, can I call you Mike?'

'I'd prefer...'

Hopley interrupted. 'Good. So, is this where you've been for the last couple of weeks? Jesus! It stinks.'

'Nice of you to say so,' said Dean sarcastically, 'but I didn't have much choice. I was already here when the siren sounded.'

Hopley looked toward the ceiling as if he could see through into the room above. Bumps, growls, squeals and yelps echoed dully from the public bar.

'Those dogs will rip the rats to shreds,' said Dean, shuddering at the thought.

'I hope so,' Hopley replied. 'But the rats have the numbers.'

They sat, listening to the battle above. 'Any booze down here?' asked Hopley. 'Feels like an age since I last had a tipple.'

Dean swept the torch beam around the room. One vodka bottle, two whisky, and a rum bottle littered the floor. All empty. 'It's the end of the world; I felt like drowning my sorrows,' admitted Dean, slightly embarrassed.

The ruckus above them suddenly ceased. The men looked at each other in the dim light of the torch beam, both a little nervous.

Hopley broke the silence. 'Go on then, big lad, take a look.'

'Me?' was the surprised response. 'I'd rather not if it's all the same. Let's just stay here a while; we can go back to Tesco in the morning.'

'Stuff it,' answered Hopley, 'I'll take a look.' He took the torch, switched it on and started up the stairs. When he reached the top he took a deep breath. He was holding his breath as he turned the handle, pushing the door open slightly, and wishing that he hadn't. The room was a bloodbath. He could make out the body of at least one dead rat, but he could also see the larger of the two dogs, or what was left of it. Bloody entrails snaked from its carcass, two rats enjoying the spoils of their war, eating the dead animal. Hopley pulled the door shut and staggered, using the cold plastered wall for support. When he reached the bottom of the stairwell he turned to Dean. 'I think we'd better stay here tonight,' he said. Seeing that Dean had found at least one bottle of spirit that wasn't empty, he added, 'And pass me that whisky.'

Silence descended once more on the cellar.

'I can't believe they did it. They actually did it. Dropped the bomb,' said Dean.

'Didn't surprise me at all,' Hopley confessed. 'I've been waiting for it since I was a kid.'

'Sorry? You've been waiting for this?'

'Yeah, it was so obvious that one day it would happen. I've been a "prepper" for years.'

'What, like one of those weirdos on telly? You're kidding.'

'Kept me alive, didn't it?'

'Suppose so,' Dean admitted before asking, 'Did you lose anybody?'

'Kids, twin boys. I guess they're dead. And the wife, but she took off years ago. I'd built a fallout shelter under the back garden and she went mad. Said it ruined her flower beds, that the neighbours were talking, laughing at us. Bet she was thinking I was right after all and I bet the bastard neighbours were trying to get into it a couple of weeks ago. Here.'

Hopley passed the bottle back to Dean, who groped in the darkness for a moment until he had a hold on the vessel of amber warmth. He took a massive mouthful of the liquid, shuddering as it heated his mouth and throat, then handed it back to his companion.

'What about you?' Hopley asked.

'Two daughters and my wife. She was in the office in the city centre. I know, in my heart of hearts, that she didn't escape. She knew I was here, she would've tried to get here, my daughters too.'

'I'm sorry mate,' said Hopley. 'I knew this would happen one day,' he continued after a pause. 'I expected it years ago. I spent the 6th of June 2006 in a cellar. The date, you see. Sixth day of the sixth month of the sixth year of the new millennium. Three sixes, 666. Then the 6th of June 2016 – I had the fallout shelter by then – and even though the numbers weren't quite right, I made sure I spent the day close to the shelter. And when it did happen, it fooled me. The day of the bomb was the 23rd of June 2023 – you just need to add the fucking numbers together. I didn't think.'

'Jesus!' said Dean, completely taken aback by this madness from his companion. 'You seemed like such a normal bloke, not some kind of a nutter with all this numerology bullshit!'

'It's not bullshit. How else do you account for the date? Nobody expected the bomb that day; the brink of war seemed miles off. Even I was just out shopping at Tesco.'

'Look, mate, I'm just normal. I don't do religion and I don't do prophecies. I just look after myself and my family. I'm a property developer. A successful one. I take old, rundown buildings and turn them into something desirable.'

'So how's your portfolio looking at the moment?'

'Pass that bottle back,' was all Dean could manage in response.

'Look, I'm sorry,' said Hopley. 'It just goes to show that none of it matters. The bomb doesn't discriminate. Anyone's fair game. Rich, poor, young, old, black, white, it doesn't matter. And when you're gone, nobody cares about what you had, just what you did matters.'

'Thank you, Plato,' came Dean's sarcasm-laced reply.

'Okay, don't take the piss. I don't even like motor racing.'

Dean laughed. He was certain that Hopley had really heard of the ancient Greek philosopher. 'So, what will you miss the most?' he asked.

Hopley thought for a moment. 'Live music, Southampton Football Club, beer with the lads, and books. You?'

'My family, good wine and Beethoven. So, what won't you miss?'

'Easy,' said Hopley. 'Mobile phones, virtual assistants and self-driving cars.'

'What about Facebook, or anything Simon Cowell's involved with?' Dean prompted.

'Shit, yeah, why didn't I think of that? Every cloud, hey?'

'I wouldn't go that far,' Dean said.

V. You don't have to go home, but you can't stay here

The following morning Dean was the first to speak. 'You awake, Stuart?'

'Only for about a fortnight,' Hopley replied, drowsily.

'What time is it?'

A green glow gently shone in the darkness. 'Just gone twenty-five past five,' said Hopley. 'We need to plan things. Where's the torch?'

In a repeat of the previous afternoon, Dean once again shone the torch in Hopley's face.

'Will you please stop doing that?' implored Hopley.

'Sorry. Do you want to go first?' asked Dean, shining the beam up the stairwell.

'Shit. Okay, let's go.'

Hopley led the way, once again pressing his ear to the door, to be greeted with silence. Opening the door slightly, he peered into the morning light. The room was almost devoid of living things, though not devoid of the body parts of recently living things. The iron-rich stench of blood filled the air. Flies buzzed around the gore. It seemed the rats weren't fussy about what they ate, devouring their own fallen as well as the two dogs.

'Cover your mouth and nose. Let's not hang about,' Hopley instructed as he threw the door wide open. He set off across the bar through the open front door where he gasped for fresh air. Dean followed close behind and copied the action.

Once his composure was found, Hopley said, 'I think we should go back across the tracks. We don't want to be seen entering or leaving through the main entrance.'

'Fair enough,' agreed Dean, and he started off toward the railway lines.

They reached the railway tracks and Dean once again stopped to check that nothing was coming.

'I don't think these will be getting any use for a while,' said Hopley, kicking a rail, the clang reverberating in both directions down the line. 'It's probably safe to cross,' he added with sarcasm.

Dean harrumphed and started to cross the tracks.

On a road bridge that spanned the railway lines a lone figure watched the two men. Despite the warm morning, he had a scarf wrapped around his face. It covered the burns caused by the blast, as did the gloves he also wore.

Contrary to popular scientific theory, there was no nuclear winter to follow. Quite the opposite happened. The blasts around the world damaged the ozone layer to the point that it offered little protection from the sun's rays. Exposed skin, especially damaged skin, was burnt even more.

The man watched as Hopley and Dean continued to walk across the tracks into the trees behind the loading yard, catching a glimpse as they entered the rear gates. He turned and crossed the road between two crashed cars, the mouths of the dead drivers hanging open in disbelief.

VI. Home sweet home

Hopley and Dean worked tirelessly for the next few days. Corpses were moved, shelves were stripped, whether things were of use or not. Anything of use was moved to the staff room. Everything was loaded into containers that stood empty in the yard.

They cleaned out the cold store, which would act as a safe room. They'd use it if they needed to hide.

In the warehouse, they made a maze of shelves and boxes, blocking direct access to both the cold store and the staff room. They memorised for themselves the path over racks and through boxes, but other people would probably give up. If they were going into the store, they'd always leave through the warehouse loading bays, walk across the railway lines, double-back over the road bridge and enter from the front. They'd stack what they needed next to the now shut door at the back of the store, then leave empty-handed and reverse their journey back to the loading bay.

Anybody watching would think they'd left empty-handed and not bother going into the store. And they were being watched; every day. The scarf-faced man watched from the treeline opposite the loading yard gates. He had companions who were eager to take the supermarket for themselves. Meanwhile, the rats ate voraciously on dead shoppers, their usual crepuscular habits being forgotten, for they now realised how weak mankind was.

Hopley had gathered all the USB-powered devices he could find in the store, including power banks. He was especially interested in solar-chargeable devices, which could charge in the sun during the day and provide power to lights, phones and other devices. The men often checked their phones in vain for a signal or a message, anything. But mostly, phones were used for playing music.

July rolled into August. One lonely, desolate day merged into the next. Compared to most, the two men were living in the lap of luxury with food, water, shelter, light, over-the-counter medicines and music. The rats, however, were getting a bit more adventurous. They were entering the store, raiding the food stores. They were also showing more interest in the two men, noses twitching and mouths salivating when the humans, the live meat, was near to them. The dead had given them a food they'd not experienced before. And now they had a taste for it.

VII. I'm not one to say I …

Hopley and Dean sat at a table in the staff room discussing plans for the future. A bottle of whisky in front of each of them. Hopley had a notepad and pen.

'Right, options,' Hopley prompted. 'We can't stay here forever. Yes, we're okay for now. Plenty of supplies and all,

MARK A. SMART

but they'll run out at some point and the place is hardly secure.' He spun his pen in his fingers a few times before it slipped out of his grip and clattered on the table. Sighing, he picked it up and started the twirling process again. 'We need somewhere with power. Somewhere we can defend. Somewhere people would ignore.'

Dean grabbed his bottle and unscrewed the cap. He took a mouthful and gazed at the label on the bottle, deep in thought. 'I think I've got just the place,' he announced.

'Really?' asked Hopley.

'Yeah, it's a farm about seven or eight miles south of here.' He took another sip of whisky; Hopley followed suit. 'Warren Farm, I think it's called. Set back, defendable. It's got a windmill, no a wind turbine,' he corrected himself.

'Nice one, Mike,' said Hopley. 'Okay, we'll need to reccy it first, see if it's empty, and if not, try to play to the owner's more charitable side with the promise of supplies. We've got a lot of stuff here to barter with.'

'Agreed. We're going to need transport. A van or lorry.'

'A tractor would probably be better, go straight across the fields. The roads are a mess and nobody's going to be tidying them up any time soon.' Hopley leaned back and put his hands behind his head, gazing at the ceiling, at the patterns in the somehow-still-intact polystyrene tiles that looked like they were made by burrowing insects.

'Bikes,' said Dean. 'We find a couple of bikes and ride there.'

Hopley leaned forward again, arms now resting on the table. He pointed at Dean and smiled. 'That, my friend, is a good idea.'

Their reverie was interrupted by a sudden noise from the warehouse.

'Grab a weapon,' Hopley instructed.

'Wh, wh, what's going on?' Dean asked as he stood and grabbed the first knife he saw.

'I think we're being invaded,' Hopley replied as he grabbed a meat cleaver. 'Out of the fire escape and into the cold room from the yard, okay?'

'Okay, I'm right behind you.'

'If we get split up for any reason, keep going. If you can't get to the cold room, head to the pub.'

The plan fell apart the moment it was put into action as two men burst into the staff room, one wielding a baseball bat, the other swinging a bicycle chain. Before Hopley or Dean had a chance to react, the man with the chain had swung his arm, knocking the knife from Dean's hand. The man with the baseball bat covered Hopley, batting the meat cleaver from his hand and following up with a blow behind the knees. Hopley's legs crumpled beneath him as he fell to the floor. Dean raised his hands in surrender as a third man entered the room. Despite the heat, he wore a scarf around his face and gloves on his hands. In one hand he carried a steel golf club. As a weapon it was simple enough and lethal in the right hands.

Hopley stood and was forced into a chair by the bat-wielding man. The man with the chain grabbed Dean and thrust him into the seat next to Hopley.

Scarf-face spoke and waved the golf club around the room to indicate the subject of his words. 'This is now mine.' He had a raspy voice that sounded like his larynx had been damaged beyond repair, which is exactly what had happened when he was hit by the heatwave during the initial blast.

'All yours,' said Dean.

Hopley glared at him. 'No fucking way,' he declared, gaze still on Dean.

Scarf-face unwound the scarf from his head. Hopley was repulsed by the sight.

How the hell had this guy survived?

Dean gagged, struggling not to throw up.

Scarf-face looked like he'd been doused in petrol and then been lit up. What skin was left was flaking, dry and starting to rot.

Hopley suddenly stood, thrusting his chair backwards into the legs of baseball-bat-man, who stumbled, surprised by the sudden action. Now standing, Hopley swung a right hook with everything he had, turning his body a full one hundred and eighty degrees to connect with his assailant's chin. The other man was out cold, slumping to the floor.

Scarf-face started swinging his golf club in an arc in front of him as he approached Hopley. The golf club was a six iron. The figure '6' was embossed in the metal of its head. Hopley saw the embossed number just before the head of the club connected with his skull. Hopley somehow remained standing as Scarf-face pulled back the club to strike Hopley's head for a second time but with greater force. Club head and skull connected with a sickening crack and Hopley fell to the floor. Scarf-face stood over the prone Hopley, golf club fully raised, ready to rain down a third and final blow to Hopley's skull with all his strength.

Hopley knew the third blow to his skull would be a fatal one. *How could it not be? Three sixes. The three sixes that bought the bomb had not claimed him, but the three sixes he faced now would.* His brain tried its best to make his voice say the words *I told you so* to Dean.

Scarf-face bought down the golf club with a force that belied his cadaverous appearance, and Hopley's skull cracked open like an egg.

THE ORNAMENT

C.J. Riley

She smiled as she placed the small ornament of a girl on the mantelpiece. She stepped back to check it was perfectly positioned. She loved it. She had nearly missed it, nestled in amongst the bric-a-brac in the charity shop. She was about to walk away when it caught her eye. It looked familiar.

The girl seemed to smile at her as she picked her up from the table. She turned the tiny doll over in her hands. It was heavier than she had imagined. With the tiny intricate facial features and attention to detail, she thought it was made from plaster or porcelain, but it felt more like clay. She ran her fingers over the detail of the little girl's apron and long pleated dress, examining her for any breaks or chips. She was perfect. From her pigtailed hair and button nose down to her tiny shoes – she didn't have one mark or scratch on her. When she took her over to the till to pay even the lady at the counter was taken with the ornament.

'What a cute little girl,' the cashier said as she carefully wrapped it up in tissue paper. 'I haven't seen her before; she must have just come in. She would have looked lovely on my dresser – lucky for you, you saw her first!'

Yes, she was lucky. Lucky that she had spotted her, lucky that she was in such good condition and lucky that the shop worker hadn't seen her first.

She stepped toward the mantle and picked her up again.

'I think I will call you Lucky,' she said quietly to the girl and stroked her head gently. The expressive clay face replied with a smile and she placed her back on the mantelpiece.

Over the next few months visitors would remark at what an unusual ornament it was, how lifelike the small facial features seemed. She would proudly take her off the mantle every day and carefully dust her. She even began holding little chats with Lucky to tell her how beautiful and special she was. She couldn't have been happier with her bargain buy.

It was soon September when she was busy preparing her house for a special visitor. She took Lucky off the mantelpiece and gave her an extra polish.

'Wait until he sees you!' she said and tapped the ornament gently on the head as she placed her back in her place. She stared at her as her thoughts wandered to her little brother.

He had spent the last two years backpacking across the world and she had missed him so much. They kept in regular contact, but that didn't stop the pain of missing him. They were extremely close, closer than most siblings because of circumstance. Terrible, horrible circumstance.

It was over eight years ago that they had lost their parents. It had been terrible to lose both of their parents together, but what was even more horrifying was the way they had died.

Their father had been an absent father. He was a successful businessman and spent most of their childhood at the office or away on business trips. Their mother had successfully managed to play the role of both parents, so they didn't notice his lack of presence. When they reached their teens, suddenly their father began to spend more time at home. He became withdrawn and would argue with their mother. He would sit up all night drinking, and he would stay at home all day in a dark room. They all knew something was wrong but he wouldn't speak about what it was to anyone. Their mother had called a doctor, but he refused to speak to him either.

Months went by and things seemed to be getting worse, until one day he got up in the morning and joined them all for breakfast. For the first time in a long time he seemed happy and relaxed. It was then that he had told them he had booked for them to go to summer camp in America. He talked animatedly as he told them all about the activities and adventures they would find there. She remembered the concerned look on her mother's face, which she'd ignored at the time because she'd been so excited.

Before they knew it, the day arrived and a taxi was there to take them to the airport. They waved goodbye to their parents. She had been so wrapped up in the journey that she nearly forgot to wave at them. She turned and saw them standing at the garden gate, her father with his arm wrapped around her mother, both smiling and waving – a picture that was forever etched in her memory. When they finally arrived at the camp they got off the bus and were greeted by the staff with devastating news. Suddenly the excitement and giddiness was replaced with fear and sadness.

Their parents were dead. Both of them.

They left camp immediately and returned back to the UK. They were met by their Godparents at the airport. Because of their age, they were spared most of the details, but growing up they learned more.

Their father had been embezzling money for years, and when people began to get suspicious it had pushed him to go into a downward spiral. As the net began to close on him, he realised that there was only one way out. That evening when his children were safely on a plane, he took a kitchen knife and stabbed his wife repeatedly and then sliced his own arteries. The neighbours had alerted the police when they had heard a commotion, but by the time they arrived all they found were two corpses.

Their Godparents had taken them in. They had no other living relatives – their mother had no siblings and their father's brother had died in a car accident some years before.

Just then the doorbell rang and she hurried to the front door. She swung her arms open and fell onto the person who was waiting on the other side.

'Wow! Let me breathe!' he said laughing and dropping his rucksack to the floor.

'I'm sorry,' she replied and smiling broadly she let go of him. 'I am just so happy to see my little brother again!' She moved out of the doorway to let him inside and he picked up his bag and entered.

'Tea? Coffee? Something stronger? Are you hungry? Can I make you a sandwich?' she garbled as he removed his coat and placed it on the hook.

'How about you give me a kiss and calm down?' he smiled at her and leaned forward to peck her cheek.

'Sorry, I am just so excited to see you! I want to hear all about it. Tell me where you have been, what you have seen. I want to know everything!' She clapped her hands excitedly and he laughed at her again.

'I will, I will – but just give me chance,' he wiped his brow.

'You look tired,' she remarked and reached forward to stroke his arm. He nodded in response.

'It's been a long journey,' he replied.

'Look, why don't you go and sit down and I will make you a nice cup of tea?' she said and ushered him into the living room.

She walked back into the living room holding two steaming mugs to find him standing by the mantelpiece holding Lucky.

'Where did you get this?' he held it up to her as she placed the mugs down onto the table.

'She's lovely, isn't she? I got her from the charity shop in town.' She walked over to him and linked her arm into his.

'She looks like...' His words trailed off as he stared intently at the ornament.

'What?' she asked and turned to face him.

'Oh, never mind,' he said and placed Lucky back onto the mantelpiece. 'I am just tired; my mind is spinning!' He plonked himself down on the sofa and sank into the seats.

He patted the seat next to him. She stared at Lucky and then at the seat. Smiling, she went over to him.

'I've missed you!' she said and squeezed his knee affectionately. He placed his hand on top of hers and returned the affection.

'I've missed a warm bed and homemade food!' he laughed and she playfully nudged him and reached forward to retrieve the hot drinks from the table.

It was hours later and the room was beginning to draw dark when they eventually finished chatting.

'I think I need to go to bed now, Sis,' he said yawning and she smiled at him.

'Lightweight!' she laughed and threw a cushion at his face. He stood up and aimed the cushion back at her and then stopped and looked over at the mantle again. She followed his gaze.

'What?' she asked and sat forward on the sofa.

'Nothing,' he said, shaking his head and throwing the cushion back at her. She skilfully caught it and stood up.

'No, you were going to say something about Lucky earlier, and you changed your mind. What is it?' she said and stepped towards the ornament.

'Lucky?' he replied and raised his eyebrows questioningly.

She picked her up and smiled.

'I have called her Lucky because I nearly walked past the table and didn't see her, and then the lady in the shop remarked that she never saw her come in, otherwise she would have bought her... so it was lucky I found her.' She gently caressed the ornament's head.

'Ok, whatever,' he replied dismissively and smirked.

'No, tell me,' she insisted. He sighed and perched on the end of the sofa.

'Ok, Ok...but don't say that I didn't try to get out of it. It will sound crazy...but then again you have named an ornament!' he laughed.

'Go on,' she urged, still holding Lucky in her hand.

'Well, she just looks like a witch's child's doll.' He shook his head and laughed. 'See, I told you it sounded crazy!' He stood up again. Her face fell and she stared at Lucky and then at her brother.

'A what?' she asked.

'It's not...it can't be...it's too young...look, just ignore me. You like it, let's just leave it at that.' He stepped towards the door.

'You can't leave it at that — what is a "witch's child's doll"?' She stared down at Lucky again. The streetlamp outside flickered on and the room was bathed in a low light.

'You won't let me go to bed until I tell you, will you?' he sighed and perched down again. 'On my travels through Europe I heard all the old folklore stories.' He coughed to clear his throat.

'Go on,' she said quietly.

'During the 16th to 18th centuries there was mass hysteria about witches...'

'The witch trials?' she interrupted and raised her eyebrow. He nodded in response.

'People were terrified, terrified of witches and terrified of being accused of being a witch. Often people just accused someone because they didn't like them. Innocent people were taken from their homes and families and then tried for being a witch – which usually resulted in the death of that person.' He cleared his throat again and she stared intently waiting for what he had to say.

'So sometimes the accused women had children, and they would take the children and imprison them away from their mothers. In some places the children would also be tried because they were seen as "Satan's offspring".' He stopped and stared at the window as the glow of the streetlight became brighter.

'That's awful,' she said quietly and shook her head.

'It's horrific, but what is even more horrific is that in some places they would just imprison the children and they would often just get left and forgotten about.' He swallowed hard as he took in the horror on his sister's face.

'It's been said that the children who were imprisoned began to make talismans made out of clay from the dungeon floors. These talismans were made to hunt down the people responsible for the deaths and imprisonment and punish them.'

185

'And you think Lucky?' she whispered and stared down at the ornament.

'I just thought she looked similar…because…well… even though the dolls have been found throughout Europe they all look the same. Same hair, same dress, same shoes….' He stepped forward and took Lucky out of her hand.

'How could they all make the same thing?' she said and stared at him, her eyes wide.

'I don't know.' He tossed the ornament in the air and she shuddered as she watched him catch it again. 'I've seen some on my travels and she does look like one.' He placed her back on the mantle.

'But she can't be? How could she be? That was hundreds of years ago. She is perfect, no cracks, no marks – she can't be that old.' She stared at Lucky. He was already walking out of the room and then he stopped and turned to her.

'Oh yeah…that's part of the "curse",' he said and rubbed his eyes. 'Until the last descendant is dead, the doll can't be broken.' He stretched and yawned and turned to leave.

'You don't really think?' she said timidly.

'Oh come on!' he laughed. 'It's just a load of rubbish! It's the usual crap of someone taking an innocent story and then embellishing it to create fear and folklore!' He stared at his sister.

'But they all look the same? They can't be broken? That is just strange. How can you explain that?' she asked him and then stared at Lucky again.

'I can't explain it – but I am sure there is some reasonable explanation somewhere. There was no such thing as witches back then and there is no such thing as curses now!'

She smiled weakly at him.

'I told you I shouldn't have said anything,' he continued. 'It's just a load of old nonsense!' He gave her a reassuring smile and walked out of the room.

She watched him as he left and she suddenly felt uneasy being alone. She tried to shake the feeling and looked at Lucky. The glow of the streetlamps cast a long bright shard of light across the room and she suddenly shuddered and hurried out of the room.

That night her dreams were filled with images of small children imprisoned in cold, dank cells. Their clothes were all tattered and worn, and she could see their skeletal arms as they scooped up clay from the floor. She watched as they methodically fashioned the little button noses and pigtails, all the while singing in low harmonised tones.

She was in the cell with them. And although they were only children, they made her feel uneasy. One child wasn't singing. That child was in the corner of the cell, frozen in position, with her face pressed to the wall. From the back, she looked like a normal girl of about eight or nine; but when she turned her head – the child seeming to detect the presence of a stranger in the cell – the face that was revealed was a hideous shock. Hollow from starvation and malnutrition, the face had eyes that seemed to have sunk into their sockets and the skin was grey and leathery.

Whilst the others continued with their work, suddenly the child in the corner rushed forward, as if the air had carried her over. She held up her bony clay covered arms and clutched something in her long thin hands. It was Lucky. The child began to smile, her eyes were twisted and black with rage. Then she began to laugh, a throaty, evil laugh.

'AAAAAGGGGGGGHHHHHHHHH!' she screamed and sat up in bed. Sweat dripped from every pore and she struggled to catch her breath.

'What the...?' The door swung open and the light switch was flicked on. Her brother stood in the doorway blinking across at her.

'Nightmare...' she gasped and bent forward holding her stomach. 'It was horrible...it felt so real....it was...' She didn't want to verbalise the dream. It was still making her uneasy and if she spoke about it, it would make her feel worse.

'I shouldn't have told you all that stuff...' he said and rubbed his face.

She managed to control her breathing and sat back in bed. It was only a dream.

'Sorry,' she said meekly and gave him an embarrassed smile.

'Alright now?' he asked.

She nodded and he turned to leave.

'It wasn't about Mum, was it?' he asked as an afterthought.

She shook her head and murmured for him to go. She hadn't had nightmares about her mother for years. That was why he had decided it would be OK for him to go backpacking.

She had suffered with the nightmares ever since she had overheard a conversation at her parents' funeral. They were talking about how ferociously her father had stabbed her mother in the neck that he had nearly decapitated her. She was instantly sick.

Each night she would dream a different dream about her mother. But every dream had two things in common – every dream would start with a version of normal everyday life, and every dream would end with a vision of her mother's mutilated corpse.

He turned back and walked over to the bed.

'You don't have them anymore, do you?' he asked concernedly. She shook her head again.

'Look, you need to talk to me if you are; remember what the doctor said?' He sat down on the bed and stared at her. His expression showed how seriously he took the situation and how great his concern was.

She had had years of therapy. She had talked and talked and talked. After a while she felt strong enough and she began to rebuild her life.

'I know,' she said and smiled at him. 'It really wasn't about Mum.' She squeezed his hand and he nodded, accepting the truthfulness of her response.

'Well, I'll get back to bed then?' he asked, making sure that it was OK with her for him to leave. She nodded.

'Light on or off?' he asked as he walked to the door.

'Off,' she replied as she snuggled back down under the duvet. The uneasiness had passed now and she was beginning to feel silly.

'Night then,' he said and closed the door behind him.

'Night,' she replied and closed her eyes.

She managed to spend the rest of the night peacefully and had no more dreams. She awoke just as it started to get light and she got up and made her way downstairs.

She was cradling her coffee in her hand as she walked into the living room. The daylight flooded the room and she stared across at Lucky. An uneasiness hit the pit of her stomach and she shook her head. It was all her imagination.

Her imagination and the silly folk stories of her travelling brother.

Just then he entered the room.

'Morning,' he smiled at her. She smiled back broadly.

It was so good to have him home. They had lived with their Godparents until they were old enough to leave home, and then they had moved in together. She didn't know any other siblings that were as close as she was with her brother. But then again, she didn't know anyone else who had been through what they had been through.

They spent the morning chatting and laughing, until they decided that the day was too nice to spend inside and decided to go out to the garden.

'These hedges need to be sorted,' he said as he surveyed the giant overgrown shrubbery.

'I know, I meant to get someone in to do it,' she replied.

'Well I'm here now, I can do it. Have you got any tools in there?' he asked, pointing towards the garden shed.

'I think so,' she replied as they made their way to the shed.

She decided to stay outside for fear of any eight-legged shed dwellers, and she watched him as he picked up a large pair of garden shears and hooked a stepladder under his arm.

She followed him back into the garden and sat down on one of the garden chairs on the lawn.

'Oh I see, I do all the work and you just take it easy!' he mocked and she waved her hands dismissively as she sat back in the chair.

She loved having him home, together again. The Indian summer sun felt pleasantly warm on her face and she closed her eyes. She was tired after her restless night and she listened to the sound of the garden shears clipping as she drifted off to sleep.

She found herself standing in a field surrounded by a crowd of people. The women were wearing bodices and long sack cloth skirts; caps adorned their heads and she could see that the faces peering out from underneath were angry. The men at their side wore various styles of hats; their shirts had billowed sleeves and their trousers were made off the same material as the ladies' skirts. They also wore the same angry facial expressions as the women. The glow of the setting sun cast a shadow across the crowd and she shivered as she felt the cold air. They all seemed to be staring straight ahead of them; some were shouting and cursing, and others were baying and jeering. She peered through the crowd to see what they were looking at. She could see a wooden structure looming above the crowd. She suddenly felt a tug on her hand and she looked down; a small child wearing a brown cloak was tugging at her arm.

'What is it?' she said.

The child kept her head down – the cloak covered her entirely except for the two small pigtails poking out. The girl pulled her forward to move her to the front of the crowd.

'What do you want?' she shouted at the child in a panicked tone.

The child ignored her and pulled her forward, pushing the crowd out of the way. She looked up and could see that the wooden structure was a gallows and that it had four empty nooses which were catching the breeze and swinging in the wind. Her heart began to race and she bit her lip.

Suddenly a well-dressed man stepped forward in front of the imposing structure. She stared down at the child. The child just pointed at the man.

The man seemed to speak, but she couldn't make out what he was saying. She strained to hear, but all she could hear was the noise of the crowd. They seemed to be getting louder and she looked around her at all the angry jeering faces. She stared at the child again and tried to release herself from the grip. She could feel panic rising in her body and she didn't want to be here. The child held on tighter and pointed at the gallows.

Three figures had appeared in three of the nooses, each wearing a cloth sack over their heads. The well-dressed man ascended the wooden steps and made his way across to the figures. His mouth moved, but still she could not make out what he was saying. He reached forward and pulled off the first sack.

Her father.

She opened her mouth to let out a scream. Silence. She tried to pull away from the child to run, but the small fingers gripped her arm tightly. The bony fingers cut into her flesh. She tried to move her head away, but it was as if it was being held in an invisible vice, forcing her to look straight ahead. She tried to close her eyes, but they wouldn't move. She had no choice but to take in the figure of her father.

He was dead. His face was grey and twisted in pain. Large lacerations adorned his wrists and legs. His lifeless eyes stared ahead, fixing their glare onto her.

The man walked over to the next person and removed the sack.

Her mother.

The noose was nestling in the gaping wound of her neck. Her eyes were wide with horror and her mouth open as if it were in mid-scream.

She tried to move again but it was useless. She was

frozen. The noise of the crowd grew louder and louder, and her heart beat so fast in her chest that it felt as if it would explode. She felt sick; she could feel the bile swelling up in her throat.

The man stepped forward and reached up to the final sack. The little girl tugged her arm and she was able to move to look down. She had removed the hood of her cloak.

Lucky.

The girl smiled, not the usual sweet smile that had sat on her mantelpiece for months, but a twisted, hateful smile. Her eyes flashed with evil and seemed to be filled with blood. She pointed forward again and just as before it felt as if an unknown presence was directing her head towards to the gallows.

The man pulled off the sack and she saw her brother. He was alive. She opened her mouth to scream.

'Noooooooooooooooo!!!!!' She awoke suddenly in the chair and shot forward.

Her sudden outburst made her brother jump, and he shook unsteadily atop of the stepladders. He desperately made to grab for anything that could steady himself, but without success.

'I'm coming,' she screamed as she lurched towards him. The stepladders shook under the momentum and then began to fall.

'Help!' he yelled as he fell to the floor. She watched as he landed face down on the grass and she ran towards him screaming.

He lay there lifeless. She crouched next to him.

'No! No! No! No! No!' she repeated over and over again. She put his hand on her shoulder and tried to turn him onto his back. She pulled and he wouldn't move.

She rubbed her hand across his back and jumped as she felt something sharp catch her hand. She looked down and saw she had a huge gash across her palm. Her eyes opened wide and she stared at the body laid in front of her.

'Get up!' she screamed and shook him. She knelt up and pulled him from the floor.

His lifeless body flopped as she pulled him up towards her. He had landed on the garden shears. The handle had been forced into the ground and he had been impaled on the sharp metal blade that stuck through his chest and out of his back. Blood pumped out onto the green grass.

She turned him over and clutched his head in her hands.

'No! Wake up!' she screamed at him.

Suddenly she felt a presence next to her. She turned and Lucky was standing beside her. She was smiling. Her wicked twisted smile.

'Why?!' she yelled at the child. The girl tilted her head to the side and glared at her with her big black eyes.

'The curse,' the child rasped and then pointed straight ahead.

She was back in the field again and staring at the gallows.

Her brother hung on the third noose, the sheers impaled in his body. His eyes wide open and full of pain, his mouth gaped open as if it were trying to catch a breath.

'Now you,' the child whispered to her.

The ground shook and the field began to whir and she found herself staring at the crowd. The crowd had changed. It was no longer full of angry men and women, shouting and jeering. It was silent. The sea of faces were now mostly women. She swallowed and winced as she felt something around her neck. Panic began to swirl through her body. She turned to see the bodies of her family swinging next to her. She tried to reach up and grab the rope, but her arms were frozen to her body. She looked back at the crowd.

Twisted, evil faces focused on her; black eyes stared at her boring into her soul. All of a sudden she heard a laugh, the twisted, throaty laugh that she had heard in her nightmare the night before. She looked down and Lucky was standing in front of her. Laughing. The crowd also then began to laugh. The evil twisted, throaty laughs swelled in her ears; the noise was unbearable. She could hear incantations mixed in with the laughter and she tried to scream. She couldn't open her mouth. She couldn't move.

Lucky stepped forward and gripped her arm tightly. She pleaded with her eyes but Lucky, still smiling, ignored her.

It was hours until someone found the grisly scene in the garden. A neighbour had been closing the curtains when he saw the lifeless body lying on the grass.

The first policeman on the scene had been physically sick when he saw the sight. The man lay with garden shears sticking out of his chest, bathed in a pool of dried blood. When he went inside to check for anyone else he was sick again when he found the lifeless body of a woman hanging from the staircase.

The whole street was in shock. That night as the streetlight flickered on everything was silent.

Except for a sudden loud crash inside the house where on a mantelpiece Lucky used to sit.

BABY'S NEW BODY

Joanie Chevalier

I

'My friends have been gossiping about a new procedure ...
it's hush, hush for now, but it'll be all the rage soon.' Baby's
rings made a disco globe star pattern on the ceiling. She'd
been doing yoga, and talking nonstop for the last half an
hour. She knew good and well that the Bridge and the
Downward-Facing Dog poses were his favorites. Not that
he would practice yoga himself – it's for sissies – but he
loved to watch.

Baby prolonged the stretches for his benefit and made
soft mewing noises. As he shaved, he stole quick glances at
the mirror and wondered why she always did yoga with her
jewelry on. And then wondered if other women did yoga
wearing only a red camisole and a thong. Probably not.

'It's a procedure where you get to pick out a new,
improved body.' She chuckled, continuing her thought.
'Now the plump can be thin and the thin can be curvy.'

Denny didn't give Baby's comment any merit of course.
It didn't even make sense. But she was a talker, this one,
and a dreamer. He'd learned that she loved drama, and
gossip. Baby loved to keep up with her celebrity friends on
the latest beauty fads and cosmetic surgeries, from
liposuction to fake boobs to buttock augmentation.

His colleagues were impressed that she was his mistress. She was a catch. After all, he'd just had his fifty-second birthday and celebrated by hosting a huge party on his yacht. He wasn't the person of interest, even though it was his birthday. Baby was the hit, as usual. She sashayed around in that skin-tight dress and those six-inch heels as if she owned the yacht. Yeah, just like the song, he thought. Perfect.

Even though her body was a little plump according to today's standards, she was sexy as hell – curvy in all the right spots. She loved to flirt and when she began to flirt with the women as well as the men, playing with their hair, her lips playfully nipping at the nape of their necks, they fell in love with her too. She even invited everyone to her thirty-second birthday party next month.

His gym visits, Botox injections and protein shakes had kept him youngish-looking and fit, but the façade was becoming harder to maintain. He loved Baby, he supposed – well, loved having her as his own in a narcissistic way – but not enough to leave his wife of twenty-two years.

'Where did you hear this mumbo-jumbo?' Denny mumbled as he wiped the shaving cream from his face with a fluffy towel. 'Sounds like science fiction.'

Baby wasn't fazed by Denny's apparent distain for her comment. She switched to the Half Moon pose, her ankle showing off her new flower vine tattoo. 'Remember Janice? We saw her at Marsha's wedding at Martha's Vineyard a couple of years ago? Well, her cousin was in the slammer and he heard it from his cellmate. Said his wife's best friend did it but nobody believed her.'

Denny laughed out loud as he knotted his tie. 'Baby, you can't believe anyone who's in prison. You should know that. Everyone knows that.'

Baby, sitting on the king-sized bed now, bored with yoga and her attempts with trying to come up with new and provocative poses, leaned back seductively and pouted her lips.

Denny never grew tired of gazing at Baby's big round boobs. Instead of feeling aroused, he was a little amused. Those titties cost him six thousand. He paid for this 4,500 sq ft condo too. The bedroom alone could be used as an apartment for a family of four.

Baby flipped herself around to lie on her stomach, her round augmented butt in the air. She reached for her cell on the nightstand and started texting, her lacquered ruby and jeweled nails making loud clicking noises. She knew his weak spot. She worked it. They both knew that she would eventually get what she wanted.

II

After Baby convinced Denny to attend the New Body consultation with her, Denny felt instantly regretful. After holding little Casey, his second grandchild, last weekend, and having thoroughly enjoyed his wife's attentions, he'd began contemplating his relationship with Baby. Sure, her body was vivacious and beautiful. The only trouble was, she showed it off to everyone. His wife, however, was the opposite. Most people wouldn't know that underneath her usual leggings and casual long-sleeved blouses, she still had a slim and firm body. Especially for being fifty years old. Joining the tennis club was a great idea.

She'd been more generous with her body lately too, offering it up to him in ways he'd only had with Baby. They'd never been adventurous in the bedroom and Darla hadn't seemed interested in trying anything new. For a moment, Denny wondered if Darla were having an affair, but she seemed so busy with the grandkids and involved with her numerous clubs. She probably didn't have any time to even think of having an affair. No, Denny didn't particularly know much about women, but standing in line at the drugstore the other day he'd seen the cover of *Cosmo* with the headline 'Sexual Peaks in Women over 50'. He now believed.

Denny knew by instinct that breaking up with Baby was going to be expensive. Staying with her was expensive too but at least he enjoyed the benefits along the way.

Earlier that day Baby had snapped when he mentioned that he'd have to get home earlier than planned that weekend. He gave no excuse. He just felt like going home and relaxing, maybe play with a grandkid. Of course, Baby was livid.

'Baby, Baby, please calm down.' Denny stood and held up his hands, palms facing Baby. He'd calmed her down before, many times, and he was used to the routine. Darla most likely knew about Baby but she'd never mentioned it. Denny had the idea that she just wanted to hold on until the affair blew over. She wasn't stupid. She'd never risk losing everything by divorcing him now.

'You don't mean that. Take a deep breath—'

'How can I take a deep breath when you don't love me anymore!' Baby shouted dramatically. She threw several decorative pillows around the room angrily and placed her hands over her face, slumping on the couch. She sobbed uncontrollably.

Denny allowed her an appropriate time to wallow in self-pity before he placed a warm hand on her bare shoulder. When she looked up at him, her false eyelashes were askew and her cheeks wet with tears.

'Please Daddy! Don't deny me!' Baby cried, using her favorite nickname for him. She suddenly lunged forward and expertly unzipped Denny's pants. He knew what to expect, they've done this a million times. She would get her way. Baby always got her way.

He closed his eyes and allowed the sensations to overcome him. The problems of the last half hour disappeared. When he looked down, she was gazing up at him seductively, like an actress in an X-rated film. She was even kneeling on one of the decorative pillows she had thrown earlier during her tantrum. Baby had a look of triumph in her eyes that only another woman would recognize. Denny didn't, wouldn't or couldn't see it.

III

'Are you sure this is the place?' Denny saw graffiti-covered buildings everywhere he turned. He didn't see any signs other people were nearby. All he saw was litter and remnants of a homeless camp with broken lawn chairs, liquor bottles, and a fire pit. A shredded tent had blown against the building as if an angry black bear had ransacked the place.

He felt vulnerable but noticed a few vehicles a couple blocks over, so he hoped there were other people around somewhere. The hairs on his head bristled and it felt like he was being watched. Denny tried to shake off the feeling of dread and regret.

Baby, oblivious to the ominousness of their surroundings, stomped her delicate high-heeled foot in frustration. 'Yes, honey. How many times do I have to tell you? This is the right place!'

'Okay, okay. Call him, would you?' Denny said in

resignation. The sooner he got this over with, the better. Get Baby taken care of and get back home. That was the plan. Earlier Baby had screamed an ultimatum: 'Get me a new body or I'll tell your wife your dirty little secret – Me!' Then, before he knew it, he ended up here.

Women! Denny had no choice for now. He'd do this one last thing for Baby and then—

'We're to wait by the door,' Baby said, her voice telling him not to mess with her. Denny flinched but didn't argue. He followed her to a steel reinforced door. Its newness and appearance of security bolted into the otherwise dilapidated building was strangely out of place.

A man in a white overcoat and a bad haircut opened the steel door and motioned them inside. They both jumped when he turned three deadbolts after the door clanged shut behind them. The couple eyed each other in puzzlement. Baby shrugged.

They walked down a short, narrow hallway to the end and stepped through a hidden doorway, which led them to an open warehouse. High above their heads they noticed a catwalk hanging by thick wires next to the row of broken windows. Baby shivered when she saw someone dressed in black step back in the shadows. Could it be her imagination? She still clenched Denny's hand. Aside from their footsteps, it was silent. The warehouse had seen more productive days.

The doctor led them to another locked door behind some crates and a partition. He took out a ring of keys for this door as well. The room beyond was a cluttered office. A steel filing cabinet with overstuffed and bulging drawers stood next to a chair piled high with medical journals. There was a small basketball hoop over an overflowing trash bin filled with wadded-up paper. The man gestured to the two chairs in front of a metal desk.

Baby picked up a carton of half-eaten doughnuts with two fingers and set them on the desk in front of her. She sat down and crossed her legs, her tight skirt riding up past her thighs.

'Hello, I'm Dr Farkis,' the doctor began as he sat across from them, digging through papers strewed across the desk. He pulled out a pair of brown readers from his lab coat pocket and perched them on the edge of his nose.

'Well, now. Well, well…' Farkis folded his hands in front of him, but changed his mind and patted the scattered papers, files and journals in search of something.

He paused in thought as he found a pen and held it over a small notepad of scratch paper. 'Mr and Mrs?' His eyebrows arched as he stared at them, waiting for an answer.

Denny cleared his throat. 'Oh, we're not—'

Baby interrupted. 'Doctor, I'm the one getting the surgery, of course.' She held out her hand and Farkis leaned over and brought it up to his lips. Baby giggled. Denny made an involuntary gagging noise.

The doctor glanced at Denny, cleared his throat, and sat back down. He continued with a thoughtful tone to his voice. 'So, you've heard about our procedure, eh?'

Denny spoke up. 'I don't know much about it—'

The doctor jumped up, startling the duo. He knocked over a Styrofoam cup, spilling its contents in the process. As the coffee dripped over the edge of the desk, the doctor continued to his destination. Baby again reached for Denny's hand and squeezed.

Behind the desk sat a freestanding blackboard full of mathematical formulas. Dr Farkis stood facing it and pondered for a few seconds before erasing a small section in the right upper corner. He proceeded to draw a thin, yet hour-glass shape representing a body, with stick arms and legs and a circle, presumably to represent the head. He took a few extra seconds to add squiggles to the top of the circle to represent hair. He placed a bold X through the head of the body, pressing the chalk down so hard the screeching noise had Baby covering her ears, forgetting about the comfort of Denny's hand.

He drew a round circle with small stick arms and legs and did the same thing, but this time placing an X through the body. He placed two arched arrows between the drawn figures, facing in opposite directions.

'Say this is you.' He pointed to the round body. 'You hate your body. You want a new body. We operate, infusing your head on the other body.' Here he pointed to the thinner drawn body. He put the chalk down and swiped his hands together to get the chalk dust off his fingers. He shrugged. 'Simple.'

Denny stood. 'What the—? You call yourself a doctor?' He tugged at Baby's arm. 'Let's get out of here! This man's a nutcase!'

'Daddy, I really, really want a new body. And you promised! The doctor explained it all to me on the phone the other day—'

Most of the time when she used her nickname for him, it got her anything she wanted. But not this time. 'What? You listened to this crazy man?' He stared at the doctor, not believing this was happening. Was he tripping in the Twilight Zone?

'You hypnotized her!' he snapped at Farkis, his mind frantic to search for a logical explanation for this absurd scene.

'No, listen to me, Denny! I heard the truth! Listen.'
Baby turned to Denny and pulled on his forearms forcing
him to sit again. 'Babe, this is real. It's a new procedure,
sure, but listen.' She took in a deep, excited breath, her eyes
bright and sparkling. 'Just think! I'll be one of the first
recipients of this ground-breaking surgery. I'll be famous!
I'll go down in history!'

'If I may...' the doctor chimed in. He walked around to
the front of the desk and half sat on its edge in front of
them, his left leg swinging. 'True, this procedure is new, but
it works. In a nutshell, we take a body of your choosing and
place your head on the body. See how easy it is?' The
doctor grinned. He held his hands out, palms up. 'Now, I
know what you're thinking. Is it legit? Yes. Please allow me
to explain. We have a team of twenty-six doctors standing
by, all of them famous the world over. They are ready. The
operation takes over thirty-two hours to perform, you
know, attaching arteries, nerves, spinal cord, etcetera, but it
can be done. We've been successful on rats and other small
animals.'

'Rats?' Denny yelped.

The doctor leaned over and placed a hand on Denny's
arm. 'Yes sir, rats. They have nerve endings similar to ours,
you know.' Farkis rolled his eyes toward the ceiling and
held his index finger in the air, thinking. He turned and
shuffled around his desk, and turned back, producing a
large black and white photo in his hand. It was a photo of
two mice, one black and one white.

What Denny saw was mind-boggling. The black rat's
head was on the white rat's body, and the white rat's head
was on the black rat's body. They each had deep, jagged,
red marks around their necks, and staples connecting their
heads to the foreign body.

Baby gasped, her right hand flying up to her neck. 'I'll...
I'll have scars!?'

'No, no, dear, beautiful lady. Only for a few months.'
Farkis reached over and drew an imaginary line across
Baby's neck. His touch was light, almost sensual. He
finished with a caress on her earlobe. 'On your follow-up
appointment, we provide free laser scar removal.'

'This is crazy!' Denny jumped up again. He paced, not
sure where to go. He didn't want to leave without Baby in
tow, but she acted like she wanted to stay. Well, she could
stay if she wanted to... alone.

He rushed to the door of the office, but when he tried
to turn the knob, it held fast. He noticed the three deadbolt
locks above it could only be unlocked with a key.

'I hate to tell you this, but once people come in, they
can't leave.' The doctor was calm as he gestured with his
chin to the locked door as if to prove his statement. 'Well,
after the head transplant surgery they can leave, of course.'
He giggled. 'And only after they've recuperated.'

Baby frowned. She almost believed the doctor's every
word and was even becoming smitten with the poised-to-
be-famous doctor. 'What are you saying, doctor?'

'I'm saying you can't leave.' Farkis acted nonchalant.
'Not now after you've heard about our little operation here.
You see, once you have the surgery, we erase your memory
of the pre-consultation. Instead, you'll think you were on a
fat farm for six weeks.' He leaned in towards them and
whispered dramatically. 'That was my idea, by the way. The
fake memory. Clever, eh?' After pausing for an appreciative
response that never came, he continued. 'Of course, you
can leave after you recover from the operation, since you
won't remember anything. And if you see anyone with a
faint scar around their neck in the future, because this is

sure to catch on, you know, you'll be conditioned to ignore it.'

Denny stopped pacing. 'Is this a joke?' His eyes were wild, like a caged animal's.

'If it's a joke, it's not funny,' Baby said. Her voice trembled and she hiccupped.

'Oh, believe me. It's not a joke.'

Farkis stood up from the desk and walked over to the wall adjacent the door. He pressed a fist-sized red button. The wall behind the chalkboard slid open. A cold blast of air swept into the room as if a freezer door had been left open.

'Follow me,' the doctor commanded. 'I'll show you the available bodies. You can choose the one you like.' He grinned, directing his comment to Baby.

'Well, as long as I don't have any long-lasting scars…' Baby commented in a soft, distant voice.

The crazy doctor turned to Denny. 'Of course, I'll need a $1.2 million deposit from you, sir. Don't worry,' he said when he noticed Denny's face became flushed with astonishment, 'Baby's given me a few of your account details…'

Before Denny could protest and insist the doctor show them out ASAP, they'd stepped inside the cold room. He saw the frozen naked bodies stacked up on a Ferris wheel-like contraption. Denny promptly fainted.

Baby stepped over him and followed the doctor. She couldn't wait to pick out her new body.

IV

When Denny came to, he was shivering and alone, half-sitting against a concrete wall. He heard muffled voices from somewhere deep within, and tilted his head to listen. He recognized the light, singsong lilt of Baby's voice, never having noticed the whiny, nasal quality it had until now.

As he pulled himself into a full sitting position, he cursed himself he hadn't broken up with Baby weeks ago. He kicked off a thin fleece blanket twisted around and between his legs. Someone must have tried to cover him up, but he couldn't recall. He groaned when his fingers skimmed over a knot on the back of his head. What had happened? He felt he was on the verge of remembering, but instinct told him not to.

He couldn't tell how long he had been out. As Denny's foggy mind recalled what had happened, a migraine came on. It felt like he'd been kicked him in the back of the head by someone and kicked in the stomach at the same time.

He gagged when sudden realization hit him.

The doctor was a mad scientist! Now he knew what he was trying to remember. Talking about taking bodies and performing head transplants? *Puleese!*

Denny shook his head, trying to clear it. When his ears honed in on a loud clanging and whirring in the distance, his survival instinct kicked in. He knew he had to do something to get out of here. What if Baby didn't want to go with him? Well, that was her problem.

Denny stood and stumbled toward the voices and the odd sounds. He couldn't go the other way, the heavy door they'd come through earlier bolted shut behind him. He felt like a slab of meat in a walk-in freezer as he walked farther down the crude, dim hallway. The farther he went, the colder the air became. His nervous breaths came out in puffs of steam, and he rubbed his hands together and blew on them.

He stopped and backed up against the wall when he heard nervous laughter.

Baby.

What the fuck? I'm knocked out and lying on cold concrete while she's giggling like a school girl?

He heard the doctor's deeper voice respond. Farkis wasn't laughing, but he did sound excited. Most likely more medical mumbo-jumbo he'd made up to impress Baby. Denny didn't know if he should be proud or disgusted with her apparent lack of judgment. What did it say about him?

'Damn it… What's going on?' He pressed forward, his legs heavy and stiff from the cold, his migraine worsening, an ice-pick pain like a Charlie horse inside his skull.

He forced himself to keep going, half running, half stumbling to his destination. Denny was desperate to get out of this eerie place. It was now or never.

After he turned a corner and came out into an opening, he blinked at the burst of bright light, but it was the large object in the center of the floor that caught his attention. His mouth dropped open.

A Ferris wheel. He blinked and rubbed his eyes, now remembering why he'd fainted. His stomach was in knots, threatening to bring up remnants of breakfast at any second. It wasn't the Ferris wheel itself that disturbed him, but the objects riding in the Ferris wheel cars.

Bodies. Bodies, each of different skin tone, hair color, shape, and gender.

He exhaled a breath he hadn't realized he'd been holding when his brain registered there were no children among the bodies. He felt a second of gratitude towards the crazy doctor for having limits.

No! he scolded himself. *Don't give him any credit! He's a monster!*

Denny crept closer to the Ferris wheel and its occupants. He fooled himself for just a moment that the occupants of the cars were dummies, ... just dummies, panic over. But, no they weren't. His mind jumped from one thought to the next, one theory and then another as he tried to rationalize what he was seeing. He couldn't quite comprehend that the bodies riding around in their continuous circle were human beings and not mannequins. Mannequins his psyche could handle, but actual people? He wondered when his meltdown would occur.

He tilted his head back to get a better view at the Ferris wheel. The cars were custom made and crude, welded onto the frame of the wheel itself. They were long and narrow, eight of them in total. The narrow ends of the troughs were open and flat so the feet and heads of the naked bodies could extend out almost comfortably, and were large enough for two bodies to lie side-by-side.

Denny reached out a shaky hand, but he was quick to pull it back. It felt like the touch shocked him. The trough was cold, almost frozen to the touch. Denny stood there numb, as if in shock. His mind went blank for a moment, the world threatening to go dark. He forced himself to blink, bringing the Ferris wheel back into focus again.

Denny shivered. This was one ride he'd never buy a ticket for.

Poor bastards.

'Ah, you're alive and well, Denny!' The doctor was in a jovial mood as he and Baby walked out from behind the Ferris wheel.

Denny grimaced in disgust. The doctor was acting like they were the best of buds meeting at a backyard barbeque, ready to share a joke and a beer.

'I was showing Baby here my wonderful design. Not everyone gets a special tour of the underbelly of the great wheel, you know!' Farkis made a grand sweeping gesture with his arm, showing off his marvelous invention. 'What do you think?'

'Really? Really?' Denny managed to spit out. 'Baby... let's go. Now!'

Denny felt disgusted with himself. All he'd managed to say were a few one and two syllable words. He was too cold to think, rubbing at his arms to try and create some warmth. His mind was spinning, thoughts bombarding through the pain in his skull at a speed too quick for him to handle. This doctor was mad. This situation was unbelievable. Where were the cops when you needed them?

His cell phone! He patted his back pocket, but there was nothing there. Had he lost it when he fainted? Had the doctor taken it from him?

This must be karma, he thought. Yes, karma for being unfaithful to his wife. He'd gotten soft in his middle age, and too comfortable with his life. But he wasn't done making millions yet. He didn't want to die.

He glanced at Baby. Why wasn't she running? Why was she hesitating, almost as if she wanted to stay?

It was then Denny noticed she wore a long, luxurious mink coat, snug and wrapped around her body. If she had been wearing diamond earrings and a necklace as well, he would've thought she was dressed up to attend a Hollywood event.

Her pupils were large and dark. She fluttered her eyelashes at Denny, but only for a few seconds before turning her eyes on the doctor. Denny knew he'd lost her when she reached out to the doctor's arm and patted it with affection.

'Don't take it personally, Dr Farkis. He doesn't mean it.'

'What? Are you insane? Baby, what's gotten into you?' Denny rushed towards her and grabbed her by the shoulders, shaking her, desperate to wake her up. 'Baby, get a grip, please!'

He hated being rough with her. Her head only came up to his shoulders, and she had always been a little bit fragile, like a porcelain doll. After all this time, having the admiration of his beautiful and sexy mistress, despite being twenty years her senior, as well as having a faithful and steadfast wife who was the mother of his children, Denny thought he'd won the lottery. He'd had the best of both worlds.

What a way to lose it all, he thought.

Now, standing in front of him, enveloped in the mink coat, Baby appeared smaller and more fragile than ever before.

'Baby, snap out it!' Denny snapped his fingers in front of her face several times for emphasis. He thought it was strange she didn't even flinch. 'What has he done to you?'

'Denny, Denny, calm down!' Farkis grabbed Denny's shoulder and shoved him away from Baby. Denny was quick to face him, arms up, knees bent, ready to fight if needed. The doctor waved his hand back at him. 'No need to get wound up, Denny. It's not good for your health, you know.'

Denny followed as the doctor backed away. Quickening his pace, Denny neared the doctor and pushed him. The doctor stumbled backwards. As the two men faced each other, the only sounds were the whirring of the Ferris wheel and the wheeze of Denny's own rapid breathing.

'Listen, Denny, we're all adults here,' the doctor said. 'Baby's decided she wants a new body. Think of the possibilities! Baby gets what she wants. Your girlfriend, beautiful—'

'Don't you see, Baby?' Denny said, pleading. 'You are beautiful! You're gorgeous!'

Baby stepped closer to Denny, tears in her eyes. 'I know what you're planning, Denny. I've known it for a long time. You're leaving me.' The tears overflowed, streaming down Baby's face. She wiped at them with the sleeve of the borrowed mink coat. 'You wouldn't leave me if you thought I was beautiful.'

'Baby, of course I find you beautiful!'

'I'm fat, Denny,' she said. 'That's the reason you want to leave me.'

'Baby, you can think what you want,' Denny sighed. 'You knew coming into this relationship I was married.'

He reached out and caressed Baby's cheek. He didn't want to be a complete asshole. He did care for her, and he had loved her once. But, everything had changed. He and Darla were now grandparents. He found he'd always loved his wife after all. He felt older, wiser. Too old to be a sugar-daddy to an insecure thirty-two-year-old woman.

'Baby, honey, you're still young. You'll find love.' He locked eyes with her, wanting to connect with her, to feel her desperation. In some respects, he felt guilty and somewhat responsible for what was happening. He rushed on before he lost her. 'Baby, please don't do this. You're beautiful as you are.'

Baby continued to wipe at her eyes, black streaks of mascara running down her cheeks. She took a deep stuttering breath, glancing at Dr Farkis. He nodded, giving her the encouragement she needed to continue.

Her face changed in an instant. The bright lights were reflected in her eyes, but those eyes remained flat and unemotional.

'Denny, I want this.'

Not only had her face aged in an instant, but her voice sounded different too.

'Pay for it, Denny,' she went on. 'You owe me that much.'

Before Denny could respond, a sudden movement caused both him and Baby to jump. It was the doctor. He had produced a gas mask from somewhere and was hooking it around his head and adjusting it snug onto his nose. Denny and Baby only had a few seconds to adjust to the shock of seeing the doctor wearing a gas mask. Hearing the doctor breathing heavy into it, they didn't notice the spray pumping out from the gas canister.

V

Farkis's friend Ted, the veterinarian, called the gas Instant Sedation. Although patients were more often than not happy to proceed with the operation, there had been occasions where they'd begin having second thoughts and thus needed an extra nudge to get going. Some people! Hadn't he told them: once they came in, they couldn't leave? The doctor sighed. Some people didn't want to listen to the details. Farkis had eventually come to the conclusion that he didn't want to waste any more of his precious time again on providing extra persuasion, and so the artificial nudge of the gas to keep patients compliant was a perfect solution.

After all, what he did was an art, and yes, he was a genius, but when would the world take notice? That was the million-dollar question.

He tapped Denny's foot to make sure he was out. Baby was a petite woman, so he was sure she was. The gas would last until he could get them both strapped onto operating tables and prepped. Then, IVs would be inserted, and anesthesia dripped into their bodies.

The doctor rubbed his hands together in glee. It was time to get started. Time to get the team in place! Denny and Baby would thank him later, approximately eight weeks from now, after they woke up with brand new bodies. He couldn't help but giggle. He was seeing his name in lights.

Soon, he told himself. Soon.

DEATH BY APPOINTMENT

A.H. Sargeant

Tuesday 15th February 1977 turned out to be a significant day in the life of Michael Hanson. Well, in a manner of speaking it did. And yet it began ordinarily enough. Until, that is, around eleven o'clock in the morning. At that moment, his secretary, having first knocked and awaited his permission, entered his office.

'Your visitor is here, Mr Hanson, shall I show her in?'

Hanson looked up in surprise. 'I didn't think I had any appointments for this morning,' he said. 'I've nothing in my diary.'

His secretary came over to his desk and opened his diary.

'You've an entry here for eleven o'clock,' she replied, 'It's in your writing. Look.' She turned the book round for him to see. 'Miss Angela D'Ath, eleven o'clock this morning. She's just arrived.'

He took the diary from her. It was his writing plain enough but he certainly didn't remember making the entry.

'It's an odd name, isn't it?' queried his secretary. 'I've never come across it before.'

Her boss nodded. 'Yes, it is strange,' he agreed, his mind more occupied with the questions of who Angela D'Ath was, what the appointment was about and why he couldn't remember having made it. He had no idea of the answers to any of the questions. 'You had better show her in. And can we have some coffee, Helen?'

His secretary made for the door. 'She's quite a looker,' she said. Hanson detected a slight smile on her face.

A moment or two later she reappeared with his visitor. 'Miss D'Ath to see you, Mr Hanson,' she announced, showing her in. Hanson thought he still detected a smile on her face.

'Miss D'Ath, please come in and sit down. It's good to see you.' Indeed, it was good to see her, he thought. She *was* quite a looker. His secretary wasn't wrong there. Miss Angela D'Ath was a very attractive young woman. Hanson guessed she'd be about thirty, maybe a little younger. Shoulder-length blonde hair, the bluest eyes he had ever seen and a figure to die for. He began to entertain lascivious thoughts regarding her. He already had a mistress, could he cope with another?

'Please sit down, Miss D'Ath.' He found himself rather uneasy in her presence. He'd always been comfortable in the company of women. He fancied himself as something of a ladies' man. Yet with this young woman, he found himself a little outside his comfort zone. 'I've asked my secretary to get us some coffee.' It was as much a question as a statement.

Angela D'Ath smiled and nodded. 'That would be nice,' she said, smiling. She had the most delightful smile. 'But I regret we shall not have time for it.'

'Not have time for a coffee?' Hanson responded, mockingly. 'Of course we'll have time for it.'

'I'm sorry, Mr Hanson,' she returned, 'but time is the one thing you don't have.'

Hanson looked at her querulously. 'I'm not sure I know what you mean.'

Miss D'Ath bent down, opened her briefcase, and took out a small notebook. From an inside page she extracted a business card which she handed to Hanson across his desk.

Hanson took the card from her and looked at it. He removed his reading glasses from his top pocket and put them on. It irritated him to admit short-sightedness in front of this young woman. He peered at the writing. *Angela D'Ath: Field Agent* it said, and then underneath, the words: *The Court of Final Appeal.* Nothing else. No telephone number, no address, nothing. He turned the card over to examine the reverse. Again nothing, it was completely blank. He looked up at Miss D'Ath and removed his glasses. 'I don't understand,' he said simply. 'The Court of Final Appeal, what does it mean?'

'It means,' she said, gently but firmly, 'that today is your last day on Earth, the day you die and your afterlife is under consideration.'

'*My afterlife? Under consideration?* What are you talking about?'

'You may consider,' she added, in the same manner as before, 'that your life has been spectacularly successful. The powers that be, however, think otherwise. Before you move on, a final decision on your fate has to be made.'

Hanson leapt to his feet. 'My life *has* been successful! He paced over to the window, seemingly unaware of all that she had said, his reaction to an apparent slur on his business acumen blinding him the rest of her comments. 'Look out here,' he said, indicating the factory premises below them, 'twelve hundred people work down there. We have another three hundred in the offices here, and another hundred or so on the road in this country and throughout the world. We are the largest supplier of office equipment in Europe and all from a small backstreet operation in London's East End less than twenty-five years ago. My life *has* been successful,' he repeated. 'Highly successful, I would say!'

'No one could doubt the success of this operation.' She had joined him at the window. 'It is your *modus operandi*, the methods you employed to achieve all this, that is being questioned. After all,' she added without rancour, 'you did start in the business by seducing the owner's daughter.'

'I married her, didn't I?' Hanson retorted.

'Because she was pregnant.'

'Be that as it may,' Hanson continued, 'but this business was going nowhere under her father until I joined him – at his insistence, I might add.'

'But only to secure his daughter's future. He did it for her sake, not yours. Not that it did her any good, not in the long term. You soon grew tired of married life and began an affair with your secretary. Your neglect, not to say the abuse of your wife, led her to kill herself.'

'That had nothing to do with it! She became depressed after losing the baby.'

'And your persistent harassment of her father had nothing to do with his death?'

'He'd been unwell for years,' responded Hanson defensively, 'and I didn't hound him out. He walked away from the business of his own accord.'

'He was a very unhappy man in his last years. And you marrying your secretary only added to his discomfort.' She examined the notebook she held in her hand. 'Yours has been a dissolute life for most of the time. Any redeeming features of your childhood, or even as a young man, have long since been swept away by the shamelessness of your adult years. Your time at university was a catalogue of seduction, debauchery and deception. You have been a liar and a cheat all your life. And don't think I was unaware of your imaginings concerning me when I first came into your office.'

Hanson said nothing but stood staring out of the window. His mind was in a whirl. Who was this young woman who had invaded his office and disturbed his composure? How did she know so much about him and about his life? He had few illusions that he was a paragon of virtue or his life exemplary, but he was no worse than others of his generation.

'Not only was your personal life degenerate, but you have much to answer for in your working life. Your relations with your colleagues and staff, not to mention your workpeople and the unions, are nothing to be proud of. You are regarded as a bully. Getting your own way is the only way. Even your competitors in the industry consider you a tyrant. And you question my role in bringing these matters before you.' She spoke as if in answer to his thoughts. 'The Power I represent is now in session debating your future. You have a future, be in no doubt, but whether in Light or Darkness is presently being determined.'

He was shocked at the sudden tone of authority in her voice. 'You speak of these things as if I were already dead and awaiting judgement.'

'You *are* already dead, Mr Hanson, and judgement is being considered. Look out there.'

He looked out of the window again and stared in disbelief. It was strangely quiet. And still. Nothing was moving. He could see cars and people but they were all stationary. The smoke from the factory chimney hung motionless in the air. So too did an aeroplane high in the sky, simply hanging there like a model in a schoolboy's bedroom. It was like looking at a picture by Lowry; lots going on but nothing happening.

'What's the matter?' he asked. 'Why is it so still? Nothing's moving.'

'That's because you are no longer in time. For you time has ceased to be. You have passed from time into eternity. I told you that you had only a little time left, did I not?'

'I don't understand. I'm not dead. Look at me, I'm only forty-eight and as fit as a fiddle.' He waved his arms about as if to emphasize the point.

'You *are* dead, Mr Hanson, look,' she turned to indicate his desk.

He followed her gaze and stood dumbstruck. He saw himself still at his desk but slumped over it. Motionless. 'But... but, how?' he asked.

'A stroke,' she replied simply, 'and a heart attack. It is not uncommon among men of your age and disposition.'

'But there was so much more I wanted to do,' he complained. 'I had plans for the future.'

'That is nearly always the plea, "not enough time",' she said, 'but your days were numbered from the moment you were born and it is time now for you to die. In time, your secretary will discover your body. You will be in eternity, beyond time.'

'Isn't *now* in time,' he asked, sarcastically.

'No,' was her response, 'this *now* is your first moment in eternity. And I see the Court has reached a judgement and determined your future.' Immediately he found himself descending as if in lift. Down through the building they went, floor by floor, office by office, all the people stationary like cardboard cut-outs, one man holding a GPO telephone receiver in mid-air, another with a Styrofoam cup pressed to his lips, secretaries with fingers poised above typewriters, all of them motionless.

'We're going down!' yelled Hanson. 'Shouldn't we be going up?'

'Not so,' replied his fair companion. 'You're going down. A very, very long way down.'

Back in 1977, Hanson's secretary knocked on his door and receiving no answer, entered anyway, carrying a tray with two cups of coffee and some biscuits on a plate.

'Oh,' she exclaimed on seeing the office empty of its visitor. Then, when she saw her boss sprawled face downward across the desk, obviously no longer alive, she screamed.

Tuesday 15th February 1977 wasn't a particularly significant day for Angela D'Ath. She had had millions of appointments like it and would have millions more to keep in the next forty years ... and beyond.

AUTHOR BIOGRAPHIES AND NOTES

These are presented here in order corresponding to the order in which the stories are printed in the book.

S.L. Powell

S.L. Powell was born in Shetland, from where she moved to the Isle of Wight via Somerset, Norfolk, Dorset, Australia and Dumfries. As an adult she moved to Oxford, where she lived on boats for many years, and now lives in a house with her husband and daughter. She combines writing with working for the University of Oxford. She has previously published a novel for young teenagers, *Fifty Fifty*.

Lewis Williams

Lewis Williams is the editor of this volume and a co-founder of Corona Books UK. His recent literary endeavours have included the insane project of writing a filthy limerick for every town in the UK which didn't already have one to call its own; the results of which were published as *The Great British Limerick Book*. He has two degrees in philosophy (which number might be considered two too many) and worked for a number of years in a number of different roles for Oxford University before his ignominious departure from its employ.

Keith Trezise

Keith Trezise lives in Warwickshire, England and amongst other things is a playwright and entertainer. His plays have been performed worldwide, with his one act play *Duplex* winning a Little Theatre Guild of Great Britain award. He has been a member of a number of bands and is currently performing with his one-man show as a guitarist and vocalist. His first novel, *Frogmorton Culpepper Saves the World*, was published by Corona Books in 2017.

Sue Eaton

As a girl growing up in Northamptonshire, Sue Eaton became fascinated by the work of authors such as Ray Bradbury, John Wyndham and Terry Nation, developing a lifelong love for a well-written psychological horror story. Now retired after years, too numerous for her to recall, of teaching children with autism, she lives in a village on the borders of Cheshire and Staffordshire. Her writing is one of many things that now occupy her time, and she has had her work broadcast on BBC Radio 4.

Wondra Vanian

Wondra Vanian grew up in Eaton Rapids, Michigan, but moved to the UK when she was twenty. She now calls Pontywaun, Wales home, where she lives with her husband and their two chinchillas, three dachshunds and an evil cat. Graduating with a degree in English Language and Literature from the Open University whilst working full-time, she now writes full-time. As well as in her own books *Pale Is the New Tan* and *A Long Time Dead*, her work has been published in numerous anthologies. She has an avid interest in the horror genre and watches a horror movie almost every night, but sleeps with the lights on.

Suzan St Maur

Suzan St Maur is the founder of the award-winning website resource HowToWriteBetter.net and is a bestselling writer of non-fiction in fields including writing for business and wedding planning. She also works extensively in the third sector, running and contributing to charities in cancer survivorship. In her lighter moments, she also writes joke books, and her volume of humorous and fairly-sweary poems, *Mischieverse*, is being published by Corona Books at the same time as this volume.

Martin S. Beckley

Martin S. Beckley is a freelance graphic designer and lives in Milton Keynes with his wife and son. In his spare he enjoys reading, writing and karate. He has had a number of short stories published in a charity magazine, two stories for 7–10-year-olds and 48 stories for up-to-6-year-olds.

T.R. Hitchman

T.R. Hitchman's first crush was on Christopher Lee. She grew up in love with the eerie stories of Edgar Allan Poe and, as a child of the eighties, was profoundly affected by being allowed to stay up late to watch *Hammer House of Horror* on TV. She has written for The Gothic Society and her acclaimed novella *The Homecoming* was published electronically in 2014. This was followed in 2016 by her debut story collection, *Child of Winter – Ten Dark and Twisted Tales*, published by Corona Books.

Rosemary Salter

Rosemary Salter is the co-founder of the University of the Third Age creative writing group in Shrewsbury, to whom she has presented newly-written short stories on an almost monthly basis for the past nine years. Her stories are regularly published in the journal of British Mensa's creative writers' group, of which she is also a member. After a long and successful career running a housing association, her main interest in life now lies in animal welfare, undertaking active roles in the work of the RSPCA, the Cinnamon Trust and the Dogs Trust.

William Quincy Belle

William Quincy Belle says he is just a guy. Nobody famous; nobody rich; just some guy who likes to periodically add his two cents worth with the hope, accounting for inflation, that $0.02 is not over-evaluating his contribution. He claims that at the heart of the writing process is some sort of (psychotic) urge to put it down on paper and likes to recite the following which so far he hasn't been able to attribute to anyone: 'A writer is an egomaniac with low self-esteem.' You will find Mr Belle's unbridled stream of consciousness floating around in cyberspace.

Philip Onions

Philip Onions lives, farms and writes at Keer Falls near Burton in Kendal. He began his farming career back in 1986 with no experience and a mortgage on a tiny piece of land which everyone thought he had overpaid for. Against the odds, he made a success of it. Building a house along the way, he and his family now farm two hundred acres.

His non-fiction book on the rare breed of sheep he farms, *Whitefaced Woodland Sheep Society Flock Profiles*, was published by Corona Books in 2017. His contribution to this volume is in part based on the forest in which he lives.

S.J. Menary

S.J. Menary studied archaeology and ancient history at the University of Birmingham, before going on to develop to a career in museums. She currently works in Oxford as a museum development officer. She has had a love of gothic horror for as long as she can remember – her favourite book is *Dracula*. She writes horror, fantasy and steampunk stories, which have been published internationally in various collections. She has also written award-winning poetry. In her spare time, she is an active member of the Sealed Knot historical re-enactment society. She lives in Rugby with her partner and two cats.

Mark A. Smart

Mark A. Smart is a software developer by day and a writer by night. He published his first novel, *Don't Reply*, in 2015, an action thriller set in London and Hampshire. His interest in horror can be traced back to the lasting impression his reading James Herbert as a teenager left on him. In his free time these days he enjoys reading, gaming and cycling, and was once a Karate champion. He lives in Leicester (which city he seems to have dropped a nuclear warhead on in his story) with his wife, Charlotte, and two children, Oliver and Emilia.

AUTHOR BIOGRAPHIES AND NOTES

C.J. Riley

C.J. Riley was born in Blackburn, Lancashire and currently lives in Kent with her partner and a variety of rescue animals. She published her first novel, *Silence Pushed*, in 2016. She loves everything macabre and enjoys nothing more than settling down to watch an old Hollywood horror movie or classic Hammer film on a dark and dreary afternoon.

Joanie Chevalier

Joanie Chevalier lives in the San Francisco Bay area with a son who won't move out and two adorable Chihuahuas who on occasion reluctantly wear decorative sweaters. Besides being an author of multiple books, she works as a legal secretary and has a growing editing business (her fun job). Her writing spans various genres, but she finds horror especially fun to write. Details of her books can be found on her website along with some short stories to read. Her favourite pastimes include camping; and the sight of bright stars, sounds of a fire crackling and the aroma of bacon frying are some of her favourite things.

A.H. Sargeant

A.H. Sargeant describes himself as 'an ancient hack, well past his sell-by date', who in a former life was an advertising copywriter, but whose work never leapt off the page into mainstream literature like that of Fay Weldon or Salman Rushdie. He later worked in marketing and in his middle-years was an aviator. Long-since retired, he has returned to his first love of writing, mainly short stories, which he considers an art-form to be cherished.

Author Websites and Twitter Accounts

Those authors who have their own websites and/or Twitter accounts are listed below.

S.L. Powell
www.slpowell.co.uk

Lewis Williams
www.lewiswilliams.com

Keith Trezise
www.keithtrezise.co.uk
@KeithTrezise

Sue Eaton
@susanea04183321

Wondra Vanian
www.wondravanian.com
@witchybelle4u2

Suzan St Maur
www.howtowritebetter.net
@SuzanStMaur

Martin S. Beckley
@martinsbeckley

T.R. Hitchman
www.trhitchman.com
@TRHitchman

AUTHOR BIOGRAPHIES AND NOTES

William Quincy Belle
www.williamquincybelle.com
@wqbelle

Philip Onions
www.keerfalls.co.uk
@PhilipOnions

S.J. Menary
www.sjmenary.wordpress.com
@sjmenary_author

Mark A. Smart
@Mark_A_Smart

Joanie Chevalier
www.joaniechevalier.com
@JoanieChevalier

Also available from Corona Books UK

Corona Books is an independent publishing company, newly established in 2015. We aim to publish the brilliant, innovative and quirky, regardless of genre. A selection of our other titles follows on the next pages. All our books are available on Amazon.co.uk and Amazon worldwide.

www.coronabooks.com

@CoronaBooksUK

Visit our website or follow us on Twitter for the latest on other and forthcoming titles. On our website you can also sign up for our free e-newsletter. We promise we won't bombard you with emails and you can unsubscribe at any time.

CORONA
BOOKS

Frogmorton Culpepper Saves the World

Keith Trezise

A new scientifically fictitious novel that makes *Hitchhiker's Guide to the Galaxy* read like a municipal guide to manhole covers?

Frogmorton Culpepper didn't wake up on the day he got fired expecting to save the world, not that week at least. He had to prove out his environmental technology experiments to his superiors first. The world had yet to provide any recognition of his genius. His mother had yet to provide any recognition of his ability to do anything. The girl of his dreams had yet to provide any recognition of his existence. Some, if not all, of that changes in *Frogmorton Culpepper Saves the World*, a work of the scientifically fictitious that if it doesn't change your life forever, will at least make you smile (a lot) .... and if you want to know why there's a picture of a cleverly-folder origami rhinoceros on the cover, all we can say is that you'll have to read the book.

Child of Winter

T.R. Hitchman

An old woman harbours a painful secret and meets a young man with a dark secret of his own; a narcissistic journalist learns that the camera can tell the truth in more ways than one; and a boy discovers horrors he never imagined when he set out to get in with the cool kids ...

Ten stories of love, loss and disappointment with a dark twist are the product of the imagination of writer, T.R. Hitchman, the new master of modern macabre.

Whitefaced Woodland Sheep Society Flock Profiles

Philip Onions

The Whitefaced Woodland is one of the larger and more distinctive hill breeds of sheep, characterised by their horns – which are heavily spiralled in rams, the quality of their wool and meat, and – as the name of the breed would suggest – their white legs and faces. It is a historic breed, and one classified by the Rare Breeds Survival Trust as being a rare breed.

The Whitefaced Woodland Sheep Society exists to preserve and promote the breed, by amongst other things keeping breeders in touch with one another and maintaining a register of pure bred sheep. Some sixteen years ago, the society began a project of compiling flock profiles – interviewing breeders and photographing their flocks – with the aims of sharing information and promoting the rare and ancient breed.

Those flock profiles are collected here together for the first time, and bring together a wealth of information (and opinion), engagingly presented and illustrated with colour photographs throughout – which will be of interest not only to Whitefaced Woodland breeders, but anyone with an interest in livestock or rare breeds.

The Great British Limerick Book

Lewis Williams

Surely it can't be done. But it has been done. For the first time in the history of mankind someone has been dedicated enough and fool enough to write a filthy limerick for every town in the UK which, unlike Leeds or Devizes, doesn't already have a classic filthy limerick to call its own.

From Land's End to John o' Groats, *The Great British Limerick Book* has a filthy limerick for your town, for your uncle's town, for your cousin's husband's ex-wife's town …. as long as it's in the UK and as long as it isn't one of those few places that are really impossible to find a rhyme for.

There are over 900 limericks in the book. A lot of them are hilarious. Most of them are very funny. All of them are filthy.

The Oxbridge Limerick Book

Lewis Williams

Presenting the very finest in vulgar humour, *The Oxbridge Limerick Book* revives the ancient and noble art of the filthy limerick, injects it with a large dose of twenty-first century humour and applies it to the venerable institutions of Oxford and Cambridge, giving every college in the two universities a filthy limerick to call its own. The results will cause hilarity and provoke outrage, with what is quite possibly the best and most original little book of filthy limericks to be published since 1928.

About the author

Lewis Williams went to Darwin College, Cambridge (for one evening, that is, in 2015 for a dinner he was invited to). On the other hand, he did genuinely work at Oxford University for a number of years. His ignominious departure from its employ had nothing whatsoever to do with his writing rude limericks concerning the place or its employees. He is the author of *The Great British Limerick Book* and *The Scottish Limerick Book*. He hasn't devoted the whole of his recent past to the art of writing filthy limericks, either. He is also up to over level 400 on Candy Crush.

77997997R00143

Made in the USA
Columbia, SC
08 October 2017